Poinciana

Jane Turner Goldsmith lived in New Caledonia during the late 1980s, an uneasy period in the political history of the country, where she witnessed events that form the background to *Poinciana*, her first novel. She is also a psychologist and writer of short stories, poetry and children's fiction. She lives in the Adelaide Hills, South Australia, with her family.

Poinciana

Jane Turner Goldsmith

**Wakefield
Press**

Wakefield Press
16 Rose Street
Mile End
South Australia 5031
www.wakefieldpress.com.au

First published 2006
Reprinted 2021

Text designed by Liz Nicholson, designBITE
Typeset by Ryan Paine, Wakefield Press
Front cover photograph by Mike Hosken, Footprint Pacifique
Back cover photograph by Andrew Goldsmith

National Library of Australia
Cataloguing-in-publication entry

Turner Goldsmith, Jane.
Poinciana.

ISBN 978 1 86254 699 8.

I. Title.

A823.4

Author's note
This is a work of fiction. Any resemblance to persons living or dead is
coincidental. There is not a daily paper called *Le Journal*, no hotel Les Alizés nor
a Boulangerie du Boulevard. To my knowledge the *tribu* of Néwé does not
exist and Panié is a fictitious location for the setting of Gaëtan's farm.
However, some of the events referred to in the novel are based on true
events, though readers familiar with New Caledonia's history will find
the sequence not strictly chronological.

For Christophe and Sebastien

In memory of Jean-Jacques

Ni vous sans nous
Ni nous sans vous

graffiti, Nouméa, 1985

Deux couleurs de peau – un même chagrin

from *Les Nouvelles Calédoniennes*, July 1988

Poinciana

Delonix regia, large spreading tropical tree, having an umbrella-shaped canopy, fern-like leaves and brilliant red flowers in early summer. Native to Madagascar, named after M. de Poinci, governor of the French West Indies in the seventeenth century. Common names: *flamboyant* (French); red fire; orange fire; flame tree; fire tree; flame of the forest.

Nouméa, New Caledonia, December 1961

The bus is crowded and smells of sweat. All the windows are open but there is no breeze to relieve the heat. A European family boards, the woman looking out of place in her tailored suit among the sea of mission dresses. With one hand she steers her two daughters through, pinching their collars together. She clutches her hand luggage in the other. Their suitcases block the aisles. It is not usual to make the trip to the international airport by local bus but there is no airline coach. People usually have their family drive them up.

The man, squashed too near the other passengers, is clearly uncomfortable and keeps jumping up.

'I'll just go and get a paper,' he says, and pushes through. In a moment he is off the bus and sauntering towards the *journaux-tabac*.

A Melanesian woman in a yellow dress smiles widely at the European woman and touches the children under their chins.

'*Mignonnes!* How old are they?'

'Just seven – *la grande* and three – *la petite*,' she says, pointing to them in turn. The two girls look up at the brown face with their large blue eyes – they are not used to being so close to strangers. Their mother is acutely conscious that theirs are the only pale faces.

The driver bounds to his seat, still shouting at high volume to his mates outside. He bangs on the side of the bus.

'*Allez*, ladies and gentlemen – *en route.*'

Pushing her two girls down at the same time as she rises, the European woman calls out.

'Wait, Monsieur – my husband is not back.'

'*Hein?* Well he'd better hurry then,' answers the driver. 'I have a rendez-vous at the hotel in La Foa.'

He is clearly supported in this plan by the majority of passengers. They cheer and jostle.

'Well, where is he then, Madame?' calls another man. 'Is this how he says goodbye?'

Much general chuckling.

The younger girl starts to shrink into her mother's skirts.

'Maman – where is Papa?' whispers the older girl.

The woman's mouth sets in a thin, grim line. She casts a look outside, then quickly returns it towards the front of the bus, keeping it above the murky rows of questioning eyes. She is not about to be publicly humiliated.

The noise in the bus diminishes to a few murmurs. Everyone waits. The whites of the driver's eyes are turned to the family, all jokes aside, respectfully attentive.

The two girls disappear into their mother's clothing. The younger one hides her face.

There is just the slightest quiver around the edges of her eyes, but the woman holds her head high. She sticks her jaw out, daring anyone to ask again.

'*Allons* – let's go. He will catch the next one.'

One

The office of the daily paper *Le Journal* was situated just below the cathedral, on the rue Sébastopol. Weaving between the double-parked cars, Catherine rehearsed her introduction: Bonjour, *je me présente* . . . yes, for 11.30 . . . I'm a little early . . . *merci*. Just seconds before she had caught a flash of herself in the chrome bumper-bar of the *deux-chevaux* that had nearly skittled her, seeing herself as others must: a woman in her mid-thirties; a tourist unused to such startling driver behaviour.

'Pardon, who?' said the receptionist, shrugging, too bored to lift her eyes. 'For Henri? He's told me nothing.'

'I'm a friend of one of Monsieur Boulez's correspondents, from Australia,' explained Catherine.

Another shrug from the receptionist. 'He's in, anyway,' she said. 'The room on the right. Just knock.'

Through the open door Catherine could see Monsieur Boulez occupied on the phone. Perhaps people didn't make appointments here, she thought, or never kept them if they did. But suddenly he beckoned her in and waved her to a chair from which she had to remove several papers before she could sit down.

Standing, Monsieur Boulez continued his phone call. Catherine's eye strayed over the mess of papers on his desk. Not a patch of clear space. Littering the surface were telephone bills, advertising blurbs and faxes, cuttings, computer disks, photos, papers with embossed crests – parking fines? speeding fines? Clearly this Monsieur Boulez mixed personal and professional life with ease. She leant forward to pry, impertinent as it was. His bills were addressed to him care of his work. Now he was fossicking around for something. His hand fell over an ashtray of black cigarette stubs. He was going to light up a *Gitane* . . .

Catherine glanced at the door, feeling her chest tighten. But no, he hadn't noticed.

He turned his back on her, still talking but now looking at the wall. At least it allowed her to observe his trousers. Nice cut. Sort of bohemian, worn with a baggy island print shirt and sandals. He managed to pull off the look of the understated intellectual convincingly, she thought. Straight out of sixties Paris maybe. Eavesdropping on his conversation, she decided, despite herself, that she quite liked his style, the emphasis he gave to argument.

'*Mais non! No! Enfin! Mais tu verras,* you will see, they are wrong!'

The clipped tone, the interjections; all creating the effect of agency and dynamism.

Finally he turned around. Catherine smiled, then realised that he wasn't even looking at her. Now he was trying to find a piece of paper. Time to go – she was starting to feel she should help him. Rising, she waved her hands in an apologetic gesture: I can see you're busy, I'll come back later. She could leave a message at reception, try to organise another time.

As she rose Monsieur Boulez started flapping at her to sit down.

'*Allez, oui,* I must go. Pierre – later,' he said and slammed down the phone.

Good.

'Madame? Can I help you?' He extended a hand and smiled as if she had just been ushered in.

'Bonjour, Monsieur B – '

'Please, Henri.'

'Of course, Henri then. I'm Catherine Piron. I can come back another time if you can't see me now.'

Henri frowned. 'I'm sorry, I don't understand. You are here now. What do you want?'

Catherine hesitated. 'We had an appointment,' she said, annoyed by the slight voice tremor she'd tried to control. 'I want to look at the archives. I'm looking for information about my father, Georges Ransan.'

'Ah, mais oui, mais oui, Madame!' Henri opened his hands to the air and brought them together with a clap. 'Of course I remember. You are the Australian, yes – or I mean, French, but living in Australia. Come. Allons.'

Clasping her just above the elbow, Henri steered Catherine forward. She stiffened but let him propel her out of the office into the humidity of Nouméa at noon. La Place des Cocotiers was a blur of red; the poincianas in full bloom. The effort of adjusting her eyes to the brightness made her dizzy. Henri conveyed her deftly across a faded zebra crossing, glaring at the cars. Where was he taking her?

'You can speak to me in French,' she said. 'I am French really.'

'You don't look it,' he replied. 'Forgive me, but those shorts . . .'

Catherine flushed. Of course she'd noticed her shorts in the bumper-bar reflection. It had been too late to turn back to her two-star hotel to fish out something else from her suitcase, to search fruitlessly for what would turn out to be a fictitious iron and board.

'Well, I've only just arrived, no time for your boutiques!'

'Of course not,' he said. He was looking ahead, but she detected the slightest impression of a dimple as he smiled. 'First, *un petit café.*'

Henri stopped at the entrance to a bistro. Its windows were open and tables spread onto the sidewalk. Just before noon and lunch was already well underway.

'Didi,' he called, rapping on the window. 'You have room for two? *En vitesse* – express lunch, you know, we have work to do, we don't sit around all day at *Le Journal!*'

He laughed, presumably at the irony of his remark.

The patron approached, his face red and beaming, eyebrows raised in mild interest.

'Of course, for you, anytime, Henri! *Allez* – be seated, *Madame.*' The emphasis was on the last word.

Catherine glanced around. At most of the tables were workers enjoying their obligatory ninety-minute lunch, or young couples. She noted, grimly, that none of the women wore shorts like hers.

'You want to know about your father?' Henri said. 'Talk to the locals. You'll find out more than in the papers. Everyone knows everyone here you see. Everyone is practically related to everyone else. Either by blood or marriage or by mistake.' He broke out laughing. 'You are probably related to half the restaurant!'

At this a few diners turned around.

Catherine smiled uncomfortably. When was the last time she'd eaten with a man she didn't know? She watched him, trying to put a label onto his agitated manner.

'Everyone sleeps with somebody's wife or cousin or something like that,' Henri was saying, *sotto voce.* 'You will see.'

He laughed and Catherine felt even more distanced. Did he as well? Sleep with everyone else's wife or cousin?

Suddenly he leant across and touched her hand. It was a natural gesture, though it came as a surprise to Catherine.

'I can see I shock you. You mustn't take me so seriously.'

Catherine looked away, pretending to search for the menu.

'A dozen oysters,' Henri ordered, as the waiter approached. 'And for you, Madame? The same?'

'Are you having lunch?' she said. 'I was – '

'You have more appointments?' Henri raised his eyebrows. 'I am keeping you?'

'No – well, yes, I – '

'You were not going to stop for lunch?'

'I wanted to go to the library. They may be able to help me there.'

'Ah, but you will find they don't open till three anyway. Come. Are you really French? I do not believe it. You must eat. You will not find a menu, if you are looking. Just order the oysters and the *plat du jour*. Here it is always good.'

'Okay,' Catherine gave in. It was early days. Her money wouldn't run out for a while.

Over the oysters, Henri at last turned his attention to the reason for her visit.

'Tell me, your father. What do you want to find out?'

'It's complicated.' Catherine stopped, trying to gauge his expression.

He was looking at her, attentive, it seemed.

'I'm trying to find out whether my father might be here – still living in Nouméa.'

'Your father was born here – lived here?'

'Not born here. My parents came when I was a baby. My mother hated it, or that's what she always said. She was so Parisian, she disliked the heat and the threat of cyclones and, I suppose, the smallness of the place, after Paris.'

'Well, I can understand that, yes.' Henri shrugged.

'You're from Paris?' She narrowed her eyes. He was hard to place. He didn't seem Parisian enough, though she couldn't have said why.

'I'm from everywhere. I was born in Algeria, but spent time in Marseilles. I know Paris. But go on, go on,' he ushered. 'You have not had contact with him for a while?'

'I always thought my father was dead.' There, she had said it.

'Oh.' He took an oyster, squeezed over some lemon, swirled it down.

'Dead,' he said, finally. 'But he is not?'

'I was always told that my father died and so my mother returned to France, because at least she had some family there.'

'And . . . this was not true? You discover this, only recently?'

Catherine looked away. 'No, it wasn't true. I've only known this last bit for the last month.'

Henri looked at her silently, weighing the emotion of her words.

'I see.'

The plate of oysters was cleared and the *plat du jour* brought in. Henri swung around on his chair and looked back into the restaurant. She followed his gaze stupidly, the heat of self-consciousness, irritation and anxiety all competing for priority. Had he lost interest already?

'Excuse me,' she blurted and stood up, too quickly.

In the bathroom she looked at herself in the mirror. Her face appeared strained, her hair lank. Hardly the self-assured look.

She'd try again. There was no way around it. He had to have the story if he was to help her.

When she returned to the table, Henri had disappeared. No, there he was at the bar, talking into Didi's phone.

'Do you need to go back?' she asked as he returned.

'No, no. I have left a message with the office.'

He looked at her, holding her eyes for perhaps a half-second longer than she expected. '*Alors* – how was he supposed to have died?' he asked, sitting down.

Catherine took a breath. 'How? Well, a heart attack. Easy enough to believe, though strange for someone so young. There's a plaque, even. But not in a church. My mother never took us. She just had a plaque in the garden, I remember seeing it when I was about seven or so, but then, there was the fire and we split up, and . . .'

'Wait a minute, wait a minute,' said Henri. 'There was a fire . . . and . . . but surely, *someone* must have known he was alive? Didn't your mother have family in France, weren't there papers?' He reached into his top pocket, took out his cigarettes, lit one up.

'My grandmother died when I was five,' Catherine said, trying not to frown at the smoke. 'I never met my grandfather, he died before I was born. We never even knew my father's people. So that's all there was. Just me, my older sister and my mother. All our papers were lost in the fire anyway. Except for some that my sister gave me just before my mother died.'

'And that was just recently too?' He had guessed.

Catherine nodded. 'My sister knew all along.' She reached for her glass but knocked it, spilling wine over the table.

It took only seconds before Didi arrived to clear it up.

'I'm sorry,' said Catherine.

'No matter, no matter.'

'So here I am,' she finished, looking back at her hands, unable to lift her eyes. She wanted to stop the story there, at the same time didn't want to lose his interest.

'Go on, go on,' Henri said. 'So those in France who knew kept it a secret from you?'

'Look, what I think happened was – my mother was a proud woman. She must have decided – rightly or wrongly – that it would be better for us to grow up with the knowledge that he was dead, rather than that he deserted us. Death was easier to explain than desertion, to friends or teachers, in those times.

I don't know what my grandmother knew, and I never will now. I suppose my mother just made the choice to support us as best she could, rather than to pursue him for financial support and so on. Perhaps. But I think she was too decisive for that. For her, he really was dead, as simple as that.'

It was a long speech. When she looked up, Henri's eyes were on her, fixed with a concentrated expression that might have been mixed with concern. He touched her hand again.

'There is more, Catherine, isn't there, to your story,' he said, simply.

Catherine withdrew her hand.

'My mother couldn't look after me and so . . . I lost touch with her, when I was only eight, for reasons I can't . . .' she stopped, took a breath. If she closed her eyes now she would see smoke and the faded motif of *fleur de lys* on the tiled floor.

'This is really the first time you have tried to find out about him?'

'Well, yes, I just accepted he was dead. When you grow up with certain knowledge, it becomes a part of your life, of who you are.'

Some of the diners were leaving now, back to work. Henri looked around.

'What did you say was his name?' he said.

'It was Ransan. Georges Ransan. My surname is different. My mother changed ours when we returned to France, but kept our birth certificates – which I thought were lost – in the box that she salvaged from the fire. So I know our name was Ransan.'

'Ransan,' he repeated. 'Doesn't mean anything to me. Didi, have you ever heard of a Georges Ransan?'

The patron approached and, frowning, pressed his fists on their table. 'Ransan, now, let's see. Anybody here know of a Georges Ransan?' he turned, addressing the room.

Catherine was startled, simultaneously embarrassed and hungry for gossip or scandal, a shred, anything.

Murmurs and shakings of heads. Catherine had a sense that a name, any name, could begin a discussion that would take on a life of its own. But nobody spoke up.

'Check the records at the *Mairie*, of course,' suggested Didi. 'You'll find all the local births, marriages, deaths and so on. Or ring up all the Ransans in the phone book. It's a small country, someone will know something.'

'Try the Société Le Nickel,' offered a young man on his way out. 'Everyone here has a connection with the mines.'

'He's right,' said Henri. 'The SLN. But Catherine, start at *Le Journal*, you can search the archives. It shouldn't be hard to find out something.' He signalled to Didi for the bill with the merest lift of his eyebrows and reached to his back pocket for his wallet. Catherine fumbled for her bag, slow to react, confused by the effect of hearing him say her name. Too late, it was not in his repertoire to expect a contribution.

Henri stood. Catherine followed his lead. He extended his hand to shake hers.

'*Enchanté*, Madame.'

'Thank you,' she said. 'You've been very generous.'

'Go and have a siesta – everyone else is. It's hot here for you foreigners, look, you are sweating!'

Catherine reddened. He was so direct, and yet, it was true, she *was* perspiring. She looked out to the square where all the shops had closed.

'Come to the office whenever you want,' Henri said, touching her arm. 'If I'm not there, ask Martine. She can show you where to find things.'

For an instant Catherine felt she should embrace him – a kiss on each cheek. Perhaps the old culture was not completely lost within her.

'I'll come soon,' she said. 'Thank you.'

Two

'*Café au lait*' she calls him, the young nurse who finds him in the wet mud on the riverbank, hours after his birth. He is too shocked to wail, would have died in the tunnel of bamboo leaves feathering gently above him.

They find the body of his mother, a young Melanesian girl not yet seventeen, a few metres up the river. Nobody remembered her at the clinic; she was never admitted. She must have died not long after childbirth, the blood just-dried about her thighs, the remnants of the afterbirth, that which was not washed downstream, strewn across the riverbank.

The body of the young girl is despatched to Nouméa where it lies for days at the morgue before its identity can be confirmed. One thing is asserted – the girl is not from the local *tribu*. No one recalls any of their clan leaving, and definitely not a young pregnant girl.

The search is slow and relies on someone coming forward. When the register of missing persons is checked it appears she might be one of two young women from Nouméa. There is no knowledge about missing persons from the *tribus* located throughout the country.

A small advertisement is placed in the newspaper appealing for information, but nothing is forthcoming. Unusual that there seems to be no connection anywhere; not a friend, not a mother, no aunt, sister or cousin. The baby's existence is not mentioned, considered a further complication. Including this detail in the description – if no one knew the girl was pregnant when she died – might throw relatives off the track.

The nurse, Ghislaine, assumes the caring role during this waiting time. She is happy to do so, and it suits the *assistante sociale*, Céline, based in Nouméa, who has more than enough problems to sort out. Céline is from Paris: a *métropolitaine*, fresh from the class of 1970 graduates from the Ecole Pratique de Service Social on the Boulevard Montparnasse. This is her first posting – the unchartered wilds of New Caledonia, France's Pacific outpost. Her job is to dispense social services, match resources with those in need, find families for orphans. Twice a year she makes the expedition to the country regions for whatever social justice this meagre allocation of time might permit.

The posting has been a total shock to the young woman. Not that the problems are qualitatively different from those she has encountered on placements in France. But she is at a loss to understand the cultural norms, not only of the European-descended New Caledonians – the *caldoches* – and the Melanesians, but of all the rest. There are Tahitians, Wallis Islanders, Indonesian, Vietnamese, Chinese – it goes on. Too many, too confusing. And it has been overwhelming to be thrown into the responsibility of decision-making with no clear supervision structure. Youth and naivety mock her when she looks in the mirror, and no solution for it. Her decisions are based on the advice of the few locals with whom she has managed to connect. When she feels really desperate, she telephones her mother in Paris.

Ghislaine lives alone up the west coast in the village of Bourail, having left her family in Nouméa to take the job at the clinic. It suits her to take on the role of foster mother, if temporarily. It gives her a sense of importance and value; fills the gap, too, left by the stillbirth of her sister Nicole's baby not three weeks earlier.

'Can you keep him until we sort out where he belongs?' It is Céline, calling Ghislaine from Nouméa.

'No problem, of course,' replies Ghislaine. 'I'm due to take some leave from work.'

Robert she calls him, after her lost nephew. She cuddles him in and whispers the name, thrilled that a series of coincidences has afforded her this special privilege. Three Christian names have to be found, following convention, since the baby is legally an orphan. Accompanied by one of the women from the village, herself a foster mother to five children – *'no more, I couldn't take any more'* – Ghislaine registers his name at the *Mairie* of Bourail. Robert Paul Jacques. Three names, chosen after men in her own family. She is proud to be the one to complete such formalities. The child's name would be the least of Céline's worries.

A week passes. The days take on an easy rhythm. Robert is a placid baby; he feeds well, sleeps well, is quickly comforted. Despite herself, Ghislaine starts to worry that his *tribu* will claim him, or that a foster family will be found. Will anyone come forward? They have twenty-two days to do so. It is not feasible; a woman on her own – she has to return to work and earn a living. It would not be possible, realistically, to keep the child.

But how sweet he is, how she looks forward to having her own, not that there seem to be any imminent prospects for her in that regard. She allows herself to dream a little, sitting on a bamboo chair on the little deck of her flat, the baby heavy with milk and sleep, both of them warm in the morning sun.

From inside the sound of the phone ringing disturbs her reverie.

'Ghislaine? It's Céline.'

Ghislaine's pulse quickens.

'Yes, it's me.'

'Listen, someone has come forward. She wouldn't give her name. It's a friend, she says, from the same *tribu* – but she lives in Nouméa now.'

'Oh.'

'She said she had a friend called Clémentine who disappeared some months ago. She says Clémentine fell out with her people.'

'Oh,' repeats Ghislaine. 'Did anyone – '

'Know that she was pregnant? No, not from the *tribu*. But this girl suspected. She wasn't surprised when I told her about the baby. She knew the fellow, and it was he who caused all the trouble. There was a fight, the men of the *tribu* – the girl's father, her brothers and uncles – against the boyfriend.'

'Oh.'

'Apparently he, the boyfriend, was an older man,' Céline says. There is a pause on the end of the phone. 'And he was not one of them.'

'No surprises there,' says Ghislaine. She looks down at the baby's white-coffee skin, the faint down of gold hair on his head. Straight hair, which might curl up, perhaps, or darken one day.

'Clémentine must have run away when she knew she was pregnant,' continues Céline.

'Though surely the women – '

'I'm only guessing. It must have been something like that.'

Another pause. 'So what does it mean?'

'This young girl doesn't want to tell her people. I think she's fearful or not sure what to do.'

'And so, the baby?'

'I'm worried about this fight,' says Céline. 'The men of the *tribu*. Are they likely to be violent? To accept this baby?'

'He should be returned to his *tribu* . . .' Ghislaine has to force out the words. It is true, of course, that is where he belongs. But what if . . .

'What do you think, Ghislaine?' comes the thin voice at the end of the phone. This is a situation that none of the teachers or the books at the Ecole Pratique de Service Social have taught. Too many groups, too many customs. How can she know them all? 'What do you think?' Céline continues. 'Should we tell them? The friend did not want to be identified, though I tried to convince her. I think she just wanted to find out if the girl who died was her friend. It's not even the girl's mother who is coming forward. Nothing is official, it could just be a rumour.'

Ghislaine looks down at the small form snuggling into her shoulder. He is still sleeping, his face the perfect shape of peace in the warm sunlight. The thought of handing him over tears her apart, inevitable as it is.

'I would love to keep him,' she blurts. 'But I couldn't, I'm on my own.'

'Of course, of course,' Céline continues. 'How would her death be explained if they didn't know about the birth? What would they think?'

'She died of blood loss. That's what's on the medical certificate. There's no mention of the baby.'

'Yes, but they would ask questions.'

'Sometimes they don't. We don't even know if it's them, anyway.'

'It's better, isn't it?' Céline's voice has a tremor, a pleading quality to it. Convincing herself that it is the right, or at least the most practical, decision.

'It's better, it's better,' replies Ghislaine, her voice wavering. She pulls the little form close into her, even more tightly. 'We'll find you a family,' she whispers. 'Somewhere nearby, so your aunt can visit all the time.'

The early years are turbulent, and Robert learns to listen carefully. He knows the step of a man returning with too much beer, the scuttling of the womenfolk, the whining of the dogs. Nowhere is ever really safe. Darkness is refuge, and he learns to close his eyes, for fear that the whites will show.

His first foster family has too many children and dogs sharing the quarters. He lies in his bassinet all day, a feeding bottle with a honey-dipped teat tied up at the side, tilting down to his mouth. When Céline, on her third six-monthly visit, sees his rotten, yellow teeth, she arranges for him to be removed within twenty-four hours. Not only are the next family similarly neglectful, they beat him if he wets the bed, which he does every night, or when he fights the others for the last crust of bread.

By the age of three Robert is again uprooted, this time to the family who will see him through.

Three

Catherine decided to take the local bus back to the hotel. A siesta was a good idea. The conversation with Henri had drained her; the effort of trying to appear assured with a perfect stranger. She could never relax at the best of times, was rarely as casual as everyone else appeared here. Or it seemed that way to her.

But at least it had advanced her search a little. Henri *had* invited her to come back and look through the archives. He'd seemed so predictably French, not that she could place a finger on what that meant. Over-confident, a little brash. But he *had* given her his attention – even if only because she was a foreigner, or as a kind of curiosity; half-French, but not really.

At the station she found the bus heading to the beaches, and boarded, feeling conspicuously like a tourist in her wide-brimmed hat and unfashionable shorts.

Pairs of Melanesian women filled the seats. They smiled at her as she moved down the aisle, shifting aside their bags. She was conscious of being the only white person on the bus, not that anybody seemed to mind. Their quiet conversations, what she could overhear, revolved around their health, their work, their children. Many were employed as domestics in hotels or households.

Catherine took a seat by the window and leant against it, looking out. The colours merged together, mostly blue, white and green, the occasional flash of red or the yellow of hibiscus or frangipani. They passed empty market stalls, all closed by this time of day. A splash of recognition. Had she been here before, or was it just a feeling? She might have gone to the markets early in the morning. But with whom? Not with Maman.

Two women hailed the bus. One in her twenties, accompanied by a much older woman, perhaps her grandmother. The older woman's face looked Melanesian, with her brown skin and broad nose, yet at the same time her almond eyes suggested Vietnamese or Chinese heritage. She passed Catherine and paused, partly to shift her bag along and almost, it seemed, in appraisal of the new face. She smiled. It was a benevolent, wise smile, a smile that declared the insignificance of their differences in age and culture. Catherine smiled back, touched by the gesture.

The two women moved to the back of the bus and sat in silence for the rest of the journey. At Catherine's hotel they descended. Perhaps the young woman worked at the hotel and the older woman had recognised Catherine from the neighbourhood, not that she had been there long. She waved to them as they started climbing the hill, the older woman shuffling a few steps behind.

The hotel was right on the beach, with a room overlooking the Baie des Citrons. Modest, no elevator or air-conditioning, but the overhead fans beat comfortingly and the breeze blew in the organza curtains. She stepped out onto the balcony to take in the view. It was a languid scene, bodies parked like rows of sausages on a barbeque, bronzing in the afternoon heat. No sensible hats or sunscreen.

She stood observing a group of lithe, olive-skinned young

men play a game of informal volleyball. What was such a group doing at the beach on a weekday afternoon? They looked like university students – or, that was probably it – young men doing their military service. How rare, she mused, back home, to see so many toned, fit men.

As she watched, one of the men dropped out of the game and moved towards a bronzed body. He squatted down. He seemed to be tickling the nape of the woman's neck. She lifted her head, teased from sleep, then adjusted her body to face him, looking into his face. As the man spoke his hand stroked her hair.

Besotted, thought Catherine, and felt a twinge of a memory; something both known and lost.

She stepped back inside and sat for a long time on the bed, her thoughts returning to the lunch experience and what, if anything, it foreshadowed.

And then, because she was finally alone, she let herself mould into the bed, allowing herself to feel – the doubt of the past, apprehension, memories of pain, a splinter of hope.

It is dark but the light is rising; it must be early morning. I am a sleepy bundle on someone's back – is it my father's? I can feel only the solidness of his back, the muscles so hard it is like being carried on a board. We are walking. Where are we going? Where am I? The road rises up to us, the black of the sky merging into it. It is as if I am floating in ink, only the yellow of the street-lamps cutting through. Where is my mother, my sister? Where is home?

The smell of baking fills the air; warm bread, we must be near the boulangerie. Now I can hear the hiss and clank of machinery, the blades wincing and turning. Why are we out so late? I can feel light rain, I hear a dog yelping as he's kicked from a bin.

I am on a turtle's carapace, so far from me is this man.

Then I am in bed. I think how curious is the dark; so unfamiliar, yet known. Darkness is the sound of crockery being tipped, a glass chinking, the anticipation of a footstep at the door. The smell of grease from dinner. My mother's grimness, a question asked. I can hear the melody of speech but no words; only an answer, a monosyllable. Disagreement. The notes, rising and falling as the common ground is travelled and negotiated and compromise stretched taut like a skin. There is no moon, no reference. I know the bunk bed by the feel of the barrier that would prevent me from falling. I must be above, my sister below. It doesn't make sense, she is older.

She is probably being punished.

Tonight there is no wind to part the curtains, nothing that might let in a chink, a flimsy beam of light.

There are no answers in this darkness.

A sharp thought woke Catherine. She would check the phone book. The digital clock by her bed blinked five o'clock.

There were three Ransans, none with the initial G. What was she expecting anyway? A second wife? A brother?

He must have had a mother, or a brother or something? The question she put to her mother when she was about seven. Always met with pursed lips and no reply, a set face, eyes of flint. You weren't supposed to ask. This way, slowly, he was walled out of existence.

Catherine picked up the receiver and dialled quickly, overcoming her hesitation.

'*Allô oui?*'

'Oh, good evening, Monsieur. My name is Catherine Piron, I am trying to reach a Georges Ransan and I wondered – '

'Georges Ransan, I'm sorry, that is not us, we are Albert Ransan here, you have the wrong number.'

'I know, please excuse me but I'm trying to find out any information about Georges Ransan. You wouldn't happen to know of this person?'

'I'm sorry, Madame, I don't know him.'

By the third call she was primed to expect failure. And then the response at the end of the line startled her.

'Yes, Georges, that's me, but who is it please?'

Her head was thudding. Suddenly it didn't make sense.

'It is?' she breathed, almost a whisper. '*Georges*? Georges Ransan?'

'Well strictly, Philippe Georges, but who is this, please?'

'Oh, I thought . . . this is Catherine Piron,' she followed, recovering.

The next pause was interminable.

'I'm sorry, I do not know a Catherine Piron. Perhaps you have the wrong number, or the wrong person.'

'Oh, yes of course,' she said. 'Please excuse me for disturbing you. I'm looking for my father, Georges Ransan, who I haven't seen for many years, but who I know lived here.'

'I'm sorry. I didn't know I had a namesake. But I am sure I don't have a daughter, at least not that I know of, and certainly not – could we say – a contemporary.' An embarrassed throat-clearing at the end of the line. Only now did she notice the timbre of his voice – a young man. How stupid of her.

She flicked through the pages of the telephone book. What was she going to do? Phone everyone else in the town? She dropped the book and fell back on the bed.

Four

When she closes her eyes she is there, Paris, in the fuggy arrivals hall at Charles de Gaulle, waiting for her sister to recognise her.

'Catherine – but yes, it's you, finally!'

Vivi embraces her, but keeps it to a kiss on each cheek. Catherine feels large and cumbersome in comparison, or perhaps it's just strange after all this time. Vivi, holding her back, throwing her back to childhood.

'Catherine, *ma petite*, it's good to see you. Vincent is parking the car. You know it is terrible to find parking.'

Always this strange créole of French and English.

'The flight was long,' says Catherine. 'As usual, I hardly slept.'

'Terrible, terrible,' says Vivi. She makes little tutting noises and shakes her head.

They never travel, thinks Catherine, so how would she know?

'*Désolé*, Catherine, the parking, as usual.' Vincent appearing. Balding, monolithic. Gallic.

'*Comment vas-tu ma belle soeur?* Let me embrace you.' Two more pecks, one on each cheek.

At least you knew where to kiss people here, always a problem at home.

Then the traffic, coming from all angles. Everything terrible, scandalous, frightful. The nation, their businesses, their apartments in the country, the divorces of their friends.

'Listen, Catherine.' The message on the answering machine, the prelude to it all. 'We 'ave 'ad enough now. Maman becomes *insupportable*. Unbearable, I say. It is enough for us I tell you. Vincent cannot cope any more. This time she is wandering the streets. We 'ad the police. We know she is crazy but what to do, what to do now? I ring again.'

There we are in the photo – Vivi's head and pony-tail a blur of movement. She could never sit still for a photo. There is my mother's hand, also a blur as she tries to stay her daughter for a moment in time. There I am, a little apart from them – my hands in my lap, my ankles neatly crossed . . .

'Tomorrow,' Vivi says. 'Tomorrow we visit the homes. I show you and we decide.'

It is late autumn and we are driving at an unsafe speed around the squares of Paris – stone and edifice and awnings flash by and the cars keep coming at me from all sides. We are at L'Etoile now and I am sure Vivi is going around for the second time just to scare me, or maybe she is trying to impress. I don't understand the traffic rules or whether there are any when suddenly Vivi brakes and I jolt forward. What now? *'Les fleurs!'* she cries as if she has been pinched. 'We forget the flowers!'

I am dismayed at the inconvenience her sudden braking will cause the driver behind. In the side mirror I see him expressing his offence in the usual spirited way. Glaring into her rear-vision mirror, Vivi swears at him. Catching his *bras d'honneur* she tries the charm tactic and a fake smile. *'Allez*, Monsieur, be nice,' but

I see he is no more impressed with this. A sudden reversal and change of lanes.

'Can't we buy flowers closer to the home? We'll never get a park in the centre of Paris,' I protest.

'But you are joking!' cries Vivi in disdain. 'You want to buy them in a supermarket, yes? No, we go to Les Lilas sont Fleuris, of course, there is no other in Paris.'

Vivi surges forward in the new lane. She reminds me of some childhood cartoon figure in a vintage car, lurching and swaying on roads that seem narrower than any cartoon roads. 'Slow down, Vivi, please, for God's sake, or I'm jumping out. Stop! I'm going to jump out right now!' Vivi's face has a gleaming look and I am certain now that she is putting on a Parisian show for my benefit.

'Not far, not far. *Merci*, Monsieur,' she says as she glides past a chugging Renault. 'Should be banished from Paris – imagine! *Mais vraiment, ils exagèrent!*' Then: 'Here we are!'

Vivi double parks, leaves her hazard lights flashing and charges into Les Lilas sont Fleuris. I sink down in the front seat, sure any minute the gendarmes will bear down on me and I'll be towed away. 'But my sister, Monsieur, I tried to stop her!' And they will get out their notebooks and write out the fine.

Thank God, Vivi sweeps out at last like a bride carrying an enormous bouquet of white lilies. I wonder if Maman expects this every time or whether I can be excused the flamboyance, being half-Australian. The lilies look funereal, I would have bought her lisianthus, but perhaps lisianthus would be considered funereal here. Vivi grates into first gear again and we spin away. Everything spins, my head, my life, this bizarre creature beside me who is my sister. I wonder if we will ever arrive alive to visit Maman.

'It's not Catherine,' declares Marthe. 'Catherine is much younger. She doesn't have wrinkles.'

'*Mais oui*, Maman, of course it is her. Look at her face.'

'I don't have many wrinkles,' says Catherine. 'Not as many as Vivi if you look closely. Vivi just covers hers better.'

Marthe peers at her daughter's face.

'Pah! It is a trick you are playing, Edwige. You want me to sign papers, you pretend she is your sister.'

Catherine walks to the window. Down below she notes that the grounds are well kept, there is a large expanse of lawn and she can see a wheelbarrow and someone squatting, weeding the beds of delphiniums. Around the driveway a woman comes running, probably a nurse arriving late for her shift.

'We may as well leave.' Catherine's back is still turned. 'She's not going to change her mind.'

'Maman, be reasonable, at least be nice,' pleads Vivi. 'She's come all this way.'

Catherine watches the nurse hurry up the main driveway. She almost trips over the wheelbarrow, and there is a brief altercation with the gardener.

'Why should I be nice? What does she bring to me?'

'Well, those flowers for a start,' says Vivi. 'Go on, you can't say they are not beautiful, Maman.'

The rare display of support takes Catherine by surprise.

'Come on,' continues Vivi, 'tell us a story or smile at least.'

'You want a story! I'll tell you a story about this *maison des folles*. Mad, all of them, look around you, there are hundreds of stories, a million lines of poetry in their faces.' Maman gestures extravagantly and Catherine has to smile. Perhaps this is true. If they are poetry, Maman, you are pure theatre.

Marthe wags a finger in her direction.

'Who is she? What is she mumbling?'

'We had better go, if you can't be civil. Catherine is tired, she has flown a long way.'

'As you like.'

Vivi leans forward to embrace her mother, who proffers, dutifully, her dry cheeks.

'We'll see you tomorrow.'

Marthe shrugs.

Catherine is unsure. Will she embrace her?

Anger rises, suddenly, and she turns on her heels to the door. It is unfair, she knows, perhaps she should not blame Marthe, but the outrage of injustice, of rejection, stings hotly still.

'A demain, see you tomorrow.'

Marthe doesn't look at them as they depart, but turns, also, to the window. There is an officious knock at the door and a nurse, looking rushed, enters.

'Time for a bath now, shall we?' she says.

At the door, Catherine adds, though softly, 'I'll bring you some vanilla.'

Vivi drives through the darkening suburbs and the sisters do not speak. It is a long journey; if Maman stays in this home it will not be very convenient to their apartment.

Vivi stares, as if mesmerised by the automatic garage door whirring up before them.

'Vanilla? What did you mean?'

Catherine pauses before answering.

'I don't know why I thought of it. She always had it in her pantry cupboards. I remember the smell when she opened them.'

'I don't.'

'From Tahiti, I think. Long black beans, soft and squishy, she put them in the sugar.'

There is more silence as they both try to remember, try to wash colour over the bare sketch of their childhood.

The moment is over, as they see Vincent approaching, arms outstretched, *message* written over his face.

'For Catherine, upstairs on the phone,' he says. 'It is Marthe. She wants Catherine to return at once. She says, absolutely.'

'She really is crazy,' says Vivi. 'I'm not going back there now.'

'Where's the phone?' says Catherine. 'I'll call a cab.'

When Catherine arrives back at the home the lights are extinguished. She leaves the cab reluctantly, bargaining for a pick-up in half an hour. The cab squeals away and she is left looking at the front portice with its chiselled stone façade. Not very welcoming. Should she rap? She presses on the buzzer several times before she gets a response through the intercom.

'Who is it?'

'It's Madame Piron's daughter, Catherine Piron. We were just here and my mother called for me to return.'

'I'm sorry, Madame. It's too late now, everyone is asleep.'

'Yes I know, but it must be urgent for her to call me.'

'If you'd like to wait a moment I'll check on Madame.'

Before Catherine can issue a response the intercom has gone dead. After several minutes in the darkness she buzzes crossly again.

'Excuse me, but I object to having to wait here in the dark. My mother called – I think she needs to speak to me.'

'Who is it, please?'

'We've been through this! Is this someone else now?' Catherine can't help her tone rise in anger. 'I was speaking to someone just minutes ago who appears to have forgotten me. She was going to check on my mother, Madame Piron, to see if – '

'Hang on a moment, I'll see what's hap – '

'No!' Catherine shouts now, 'Just let me in, will you? My mother called about an hour ago and wanted me to come back immediately. Could you please just let me in!'

There is silence on the end of the intercom and then it crackles again. Catherine hears a conversation between the night staff. It's Madame Piron's daughter outside, yes. She's checked on Madame Piron. Madame Piron was not in her bed and was found pacing in the corridor. Says she wants to know if it is Georges, finally. But it's a woman outside, says she's her daughter.

'Georges? But he's – that's my father – he's . . .' starts Catherine, 'Excuse me, can you hear me? What is going on?'

'Excuse me, Madame. Apparently Madame was expecting a Georges.'

'Georges?' says Catherine again. 'But he's *dead*. What . . . please for God's sake can you let me in!'

Another delay. She hears fumbling of keys and the door is finally opened to her. 'Thank you, *enfin!*' She tries to rein in her frustration for fear they will close it again in her face.

Now she is face to face with the night staff, the hot sensation of accusation still flushing her cheeks.

'Can I speak with my mother, please,' Catherine insists, surprised by her own assertiveness. 'I know it's late and I'm sorry. But this is important. I may not get another chance, you see.'

Catherine looks up to see Marthe appearing down the stairs. The vision jolts her, throws her back into childhood. She and Vivi warming their nightgowns on the heater. Marthe descending the stairs, always serene at this time of night, in the secure knowledge that bedtime was five minutes away.

'It's nearly bedtime,' Catherine blurts. The two nurses have lapsed into silence.

'Time for bed, yes,' says Marthe. 'Have you kissed your father goodnight?'

Catherine feels in a trance. 'Not yet, Maman. Where is he?'

'Oh, I don't know, I don't know, he's been a long time gone.

Too long for two little girls.' Marthe shakes her head and, for a moment, looks demented and frail again.

'Maman, it's me, Catherine. Your daughter. The one you haven't seen for a long time.'

Marthe turns her eyes to her daughter. Even from a distance, Catherine is surprised that they are so clear. So blue and clear. It is so long since she has looked into her mother's eyes.

'You know who I am,' she says softly.

'Of course. It's Catherine,' says Marthe. 'You should go and get your father. He's been a long time gone.'

'Maman, Papa is dead. Remember? He died years ago. When I was little. Look at me. Come here.'

Again, her eyes. Lucid, knowing, living eyes.

'Georges didn't die,' says Marthe, not blinking.

Catherine stares. In the pause that follows she is distracted by the thought that the night staff are about to begin their official line. She can't focus on what Marthe is saying. Something is wrong. Her mother is quite lucid. She is standing here telling her that her father is not dead.

'Where is he then?' she challenges.

'At the *journaux-tabac*. Gone to get cigarettes. Smokes too much.'

'Maman . . .' Catherine takes a step towards her but Marthe shrugs away.

'Too hot, too dirty for two little girls. Bad weather. Dengue fever.'

'Excuse me, Madame,' interrupts the nurse finally. 'I'm sorry but we really can't let you stay here in the foyer all night. Have you finished your conversation, because we should lock up for the evening.'

Have I finished my conversation? thinks Catherine. No. I haven't finished my conversation.

Marthe has looked away now.

'I forgot to tell you,' she says.

'Come now, Madame Piron, we will have to let your daughter go now. Do you have a car, Madame, or do you need to call a taxi?'

'Time for bed, didn't you say?' says Marthe. 'I had better be going. These people will chase me to bed with a wooden spoon if . . .'

Catherine is watching her mother's back as she climbs the stairs, escorted by the nurse. Marthe has a straight spine, and she holds her head high. Always like that.

There is a horn blast from outside. The taxi.

Catherine steps stiffly into it. She has been unable to formulate a thank you to the night staff. She is left to her thoughts as the cab spins away into the night.

Vivi and Vincent are asleep when Catherine returns. She changes and squashes herself into an obstinate sofa bed, which sinks depressingly in the middle, more like a hammock than a bed. Probably a long time since it has been used. With all Vincent's cash can't they afford a decent guest bed? Even without the bizarre conversation at the home, it seems she is destined for a troubled night. Her thoughts turn back to her late-night experience. What had Marthe said about Georges? Confusing past and present, truth and fiction. Will she mention it to Vivi in the morning? No sense puzzling over it now.

But what else is there to think about? It is not the first time Catherine has been alone with chill thoughts, but with the vertigo of the flight, the worry about Marthe's future, and now these strange disclosures – it all seems a thousand times worse. She wants answers. Dare she wake her sister? In a second Catherine has levered herself out of the bed and padded to Vivi's bedroom door.

'Vivi?'

No answer. She taps, lightly at first, then harder. She can hear Vincent snoring on the other side.

'Vivi – I need to talk to you!'

Then there is movement, mumbling, and a sleep-infused face opens the door to her.

'What's the matter?'

'Vivi, I went back to the home.'

'Et alors?'

'I had this strange conversation with Maman. She kept telling me I should go and kiss Georges goodnight. It was bizarre. Has she gone on like that to you?'

Vivi's face stiffens out of its drowsiness. In the dim light it looks pallid, all make-up removed. This, Catherine thinks, is the true face of her sister.

'Oh God,' says Vivi, loud enough for Catherine to hear.

'What do you mean?'

'Nothing, Catherine – go to sleep, it's too late to talk. She must have been rambling. I'll tell you – talk to you – in the morning.'

'What is there to tell me?' Catherine's whisper has risen to a gruff, urgent growl. 'I mean, she obviously has dementia, but she knew what she was saying. It was so strange.'

Vivi's face has been changing slowly, from sleepy annoyance to stony grimness – just like Marthe's, when you asked questions you shouldn't.

The moment seems to stretch out for Catherine, as she watches her sister's face, tries to read its expression. The instant she registers Vivi's deception, she takes in a sharp breath and her sister – unbelievably – tries to shut the door in her face. 'Go away – let me sleep!'

'You're *lying*, aren't you!' Catherine snarls. 'What she said is *true* – Georges *didn't* die. Tell me! I *have* to know! I can't believe you're doing this to me!'

She wants to thump the door down. She hears Vincent spluttering awake. Soon he'll be there too in his stupid white pyjamas.

Vivi is still pushing against the door, crying 'Go away, go away!' Eventually she gets it shut, almost jamming Catherine's fingers. Catherine beats on the door, hears Vincent's questioning, booming voice, Vivi trying to placate: 'It's nothing, nothing, don't listen to her. It's Maman again and her craziness.'

Catherine feels she is being excluded like a school-girl bullied by prefects, shut out of the truth, of time and history, of her own life.

'Let me in! Tell me what happened! So it was all a lie? My father didn't die when you told me he did!' She is sobbing now as she beats on the door. 'Does that mean he's alive? Where is he?'

From behind the door it is Vincent now who reprimands her, like a naughty child, a toddler in a tantrum.

'Catherine, go to bed. There is nothing to say, do you hear me? We will talk in the morning. Go to bed.'

'Why hasn't anyone told *me*?' Catherine gives one more retaliatory shove against the door but Vincent has his considerable weight against it.

Finally, exhausted, she is helpless to do anything but return to her buckled, unyielding bed and the night of pounding darkness.

It does not take long to gather her belongings in the morning; she has hardly unpacked her suitcase. Her eyes are puffy and swollen; if she slept at all it was fitful, full of plane crashes and desolate landscapes. Vivi has alternated between spitting reproach and brooding remorse, finishing with 'You don't understand, it was better . . .'

The last anyone saw of Georges was at the bus station in Nouméa: Vivi confirms this much, and it is all she knows.

Catherine cannot bear to stay a moment longer. She will take the next plane back. Home is Australia now. Why had she come in the first place? They do not belong together like family should, neither they to her, nor she to them.

Booking a taxi causes a delay, as the line is constantly engaged. Vincent, perhaps ashamed at his collusion, feels an obligation to help. He offers to drive her to Charles de Gaulle. Catherine accepts impulsively in her haste to escape.

They sit, in compressed silence, awaiting the garage door. Just as Vincent accelerates to leave, Vivi's grey, still-unmade face appears, waving at them to stop. 'Here,' she says, not looking at Catherine, thrusting a sheaf of papers at her. 'From Marthe's box.'

She turns on her heel, and the banging door echoes through the basement as she exits.

'Vivi! Give it back.' Marthe's voice. I can hear it still, the sharp pinch of it, even when you were sick and mothers were supposed to comfort.

'No,' says Vivi, pouting, pirouetting. 'No, no, no.'

'This instant. Now,' says Marthe. 'Now,' she repeats, hands on hips.

'No.'

'I'll show you no,' says Marthe. In an instant she has Vivi by the ear and is frogmarching her inside. I hesitate. Is it safer to go or to stay? I risk getting swiped in the crossfire and skulk behind. It is my doll. I don't care about getting it back now. Now that things are about to blow up.

Marthe holds Vivi at arm's length with one hand and tries to wrestle the doll from her with the other. Vivi squeals as if undergoing tooth-extraction. She clings to the doll and I can see its already weakened seams straining.

'No!' I cry. 'She can have it, she can have it. I don't want it any more.'

But the fight is on to the end now. Neither yields. I can feel my cheeks stinging, I cup my hands over my ears to dull Vivi's screams. I don't want to see it. I can't watch. But I see Marthe tearing the doll free by the hair. Its stuffing flies out in an arc.

'See! See what you've done! Now it's ruined. Now no one can play with it. Are you satisfied?' Marthe is at Vivi's level, eyeballing her ferociously.

And this is the bit I remember most. She drops the doll. On the ground. I can still remember the little crack it makes when it hits, its head a little harder than its soft body. It isn't a special doll, not a very precious one. But I can still conjure its lifeless eyes and its broken neck, its immunity to pain, in a second.

Vivi has finally backed into a corner. She drops her head.

'I hope you're satisfied,' Marthe says again, and wipes her hands on her apron. She clacks off, leaving the doll bleeding on the ground.

———

The square, handwritten letter was on top of the pile of mail that awaited Catherine at work, three weeks after her precipitant return home from France. Marked simply: 'Madame Piron, Catherine, Université d'Adelaïde, Australie du Sud'. She recognised her sister's florid handwriting. No department, no street address; Vivi clearly had no such details. Inside was a black-edged card with an inscription from Monsieur and Madame Garnier, Vincent and Edwige (Vivi), regrettably announcing the passing of their beloved mother and mother-in-law, Marthe Elisabeth

Piron, born 23 May 1921, Avignon, died 30 November 1994, Paris.

No mention of Catherine, no signature, no handwritten note.

She stared at the card until it blurred out of focus. Its black lettering was ugly; too formal, too calamitous. Strangely, as if nature were in sympathy, rain started drumming on her office windows. Fickle December weather.

Less than an hour later she found herself in the sitting room of her inner-city flat, plopped on a sagging sofa, staring without inclination to move at the water dripping through the ceiling leak she had intended to have repaired during her absence. The room badly needed a paint, she found herself thinking, as a kind of abstract overlay to the numbness. The cat sniffed at her feet, as if contemplating the comfort of a lap, then decided against jumping up. The pot plants needed watering.

Some had died.

The Dean granted her special leave 'on compassionate grounds'. It was almost the end of year break, they could easily cover her for the period.

She could stay for up to three months in New Caledonia on her Australian passport. It would be easy to find a house-sitter. They might even take better care of the plants than she had. No time to give much in the way of explanation to friends.

She could always write to them later, if there was anything to find out.

Five

Dinner in the yellow kitchen is over. Dominique clears the table, the older boys help at the sink. Robert traces a 'G' over the space under his lifted plate.

'Gaëtan,' he says. 'Ga-ë-tan.' He looks up.

'That's my name,' says Gaëtan.

'How come you're called *papy*? The others all say papa.'

'I'm old. Everyone calls me *papy*. You're a *papy* when you're old and a papa when you're young.'

'How come you're old?'

'What do you mean, how come? I just am.'

'Were you always old? Were you old when I was born?'

Gaëtan pauses before answering.

'Yes, I was.'

'And so I called you *papy*, not papa?'

'You wouldn't have ever called me papa.'

'Why not?'

'I'm not your papa.'

Robert stops for a moment. He knows this, he has been told. But it suddenly sounds new to him.

'But you look after me.'

'Yes.'

'Why are you looking after me then?'

'Because – because we wanted to look after you and you didn't have anyone else to do that.'

'Why not?'

'I've told you, Bobo, your mother died, when you were a baby.'

'She's not my mother?' Robert casts a wide-eyed look at the form of Dominique, scrubbing the pots energetically at the sink.

'You know that too, my boy, she's not your mother – but she looks after you too. You call her Domi, don't you, not Maman?'

'Yes, but her name *is* Dominique,' Robert announces, logically.

'Of course, of course.'

'Where is he then?'

'Who?'

'*My* papa.'

Another pause. The dishes clank in the sink. The older boys flick each other with their tea towels.

'Ow!' yells Jean-Paul, as Didier nicks his thigh. 'That hurt!'

'Stop it you fellows, aren't you too old for carrying on like that?' Gaëtan clears his throat. *He* is too old for fights.

'So where is he then?' persists Robert.

'We don't know, *mon bonhomme.*'

The child takes this in, quietly.

'He is somewhere.'

'Yes. Probably. We don't know where.'

'Does he live near here? Could he visit?'

'*We don't know*, Robert. If we knew, maybe we could ask.'

'Do I look like him? Frédéric looks like his papa. He has red hair the same.'

Gaëtan turns away, his face tightening. 'Come and help me here, Dom,' he says.

'What does he look like?' repeats the child, as if repetition will help.

'We don't really know, Robert.' Dominique comes over. 'But I guess he must be handsome like you.'

Clearly annoyed by this, Robert raises his voice.

'But *is he like me*? Does he have curly hair or straight hair? I want to know.'

There is silence now. Dominique and Gaëtan look at each other.

'Where do I look for him?' says Robert. 'I want to see him, I want to see if he looks like me.'

Gaëtan and Dominique look away. Dominique returns to the sink, but one of the older boys has taken over. She stands in limbo, in the way.

'Hey, *Bobo*,' says Jean-Paul. 'Some fathers can't look after kids. They don't know how. It's better that they don't.'

'It's okay, okay, that's enough,' interrupts Gaëtan. 'He doesn't have to know all that.'

'I'm only trying to help. I was going to say he's better off here than having nowhere to live,' says Jean-Paul.

'He can't understand all that,' grumbles Gaëtan.

'Does he know I'm here?' tries Robert.

'No,' says Dominique. 'He doesn't.'

It is tough, but it's better than plastering over the truth. 'Robert, we think he has no idea about you. That's why you're here. You're with a family who can look after you, who really . . .' she stops. To go on would be too cruel.

'Don't worry about it,' says Gaëtan.

'She's right, don't worry, *petit bonhomme*,' says Didier. 'You'll find out. It's not worth it anyway, finding out, you'll see.'

Robert stands up at the table and takes a long look at them all, his eyes travelling from one to the other.

'Je m'en fous!' he says, his eyes filling with tears. 'I don't care what you say. I'll find him!'

'Hey, hey!' Dominique starts for him, then shrugs as he runs for the door.

'Leave, him, leave him,' says Gaëtan. 'We can't make anything better. It's better to say nothing,'

'You go, Jean-Paul,' says Dominique. 'He'll take it better from you.'

She turns to her husband. 'I don't agree with you,' she says. 'It's better to tell him the truth. What he makes up in his head is worse.'

Gaëtan shrugs. 'We don't know the truth anyway, so there's no truth to tell.'

'We think we know.'

'Yes, and what good would that do a lad of six, especially if it turns out we're wrong?'

Now Dominique shrugs. 'Maybe he should know at least as much as we know. He knows nothing about his mother.'

'And so? Do you want to mix all that up too?'

'Well, it's only normal that he should know.'

'He does know. I told him his mother died when he was a baby. And that's the truth. But he seems to have forgotten.'

'Not forgotten, I think he's starting to understand what it means.'

'You tell him more if you think he needs it. It'll only upset him though. And what if he wants to go back? What then?'

'Maybe he should be able to visit . . .'

'Visit! Throw him into total confusion.'

'Maybe it's better to grow up with the confusion while you know you're safe.'

'Well maybe,' says Gaëtan. 'What would I know?'

'I'm amazed no one has ever asked any questions from that

tribu,' continues Dominique, on another train of thought. 'I guess they just don't know.'

'Don't know or don't care? And what if it isn't that *tribu* anyway?' answers Gaëtan. 'And what are you going to do about that? Rewrite history?'

'I'm just anticipating the questions,' she answers. 'If it's not *them*, it will be *him*. He will want to know.'

'Let's deal with that when it happens,' says Gaëtan.

'It already has,' says Dominique. 'It already has.'

Six

Catherine blinked her eyes open and searched for the time. It was dark still but there was a strong smell of coffee and she could hear the sounds of people stirring below. Five o'clock.

She threw the sheet back and swung her legs over the side of the bed. Last night she had turned in early. A jog would be good.

The early light cast a rose glow over the bay. The water was calm, not that there was ever more than a ripple on this beach. She was surprised to find herself in the company of several athletes with the same idea, and soon lagged way behind a pair of lithe young men who might have been part of the group she had observed yesterday. They rounded the bend and Anse Vata bay came into view, this one a little choppier. The two men surged ahead as Catherine stopped to catch her breath. Maybe if she did this every morning, she resolved, it might make a difference to her life. A few kilos lost would hardly render her skeletal.

The smell of baking caught her as she straightened and stretched her back. If she followed it she might find breakfast. Turning in from the beach, she ran along a main boulevard, lined with cicada palms and already buzzing with morning traffic. Not

far along she encountered the source of the smell, the boulangerie, set back a little from the road, and already bursting with
morning clientele. Taking her place in the queue she viewed the
display of croissants: chocolate, raisin or almond, the range of
patisseries and baguettes in various shapes and sizes. The queue
moved past her as she vacillated between an ordinary butter
croissant and a brioche.

'*Excusez-moi*, Madame . . . *Pardonnez-moi*, Madame . . .'

'A croissant, no, make that two,' said Catherine.

The young woman serving smiled. She looked familiar. Without
thinking Catherine blurted, 'I know you from somewhere don't I?'

'We saw you yesterday on the bus,' the young woman answered.
'My grandmother says you look familiar.'

Catherine paused. The customer behind nearly stepped on her
heels.

'*Allez, poussez-vous*, Madame, we are in a hurry here.'

'Sorry, I didn't catch what you said,' Catherine continued to
the young woman. 'My French has suffered a little . . .'

'One hundred and twenty francs, please,' said the woman,
continuing to serve. '*Merci bien*, Monsieur, next, please.'

Catherine stepped out of line. Between customers she had a
punctuated conversation with the young woman.

'I must have a familiar face. People always tell me.'

'Is this your first time in Nouméa?'

'Not really. I lived here when I was younger.'

'As a child?'

'Yes . . . yes, oh – I'm holding you up. Catherine Piron, anyway,
is my name, and yours?'

'Hélène. My grandmother is Louise.'

'Nice to meet you. Perhaps I'll see you again.'

Back out onto the street, Catherine sprinted all the way back
to the hotel.

After Christmas that year another boy comes to live with them. A little younger than Robert, aged about five, maybe older. His face is pinched and his eyes sag. Felix wets the bed every night, which makes two of them. Since the others complain they are both stuck out to sleep on a mattress in the closed-in verandah, where the windows are without shutters, to tremble together at the huge moon and the garrotted wailing of the pigeons.

Every morning Dominique shakes them out of bundled, warm sleep onto the tiles.

'Again! What do you boys drink to make you piss so much?'

Dominique grumbles, but it is a resigned grumble that expresses the tiresomeness as well as the inevitability of their condition.

'We'll try not to again, *Mam*.'

At these times Robert calls her *Mam*, and Felix takes his lead, appealing to her generous maternal propensity to forgive.

Felix stays for a year, enough time to become attached to Robert, and then leaves as suddenly as he came. His mother has changed her mind and decided against giving him up for adoption. She's come through a difficult year, and now Felix has to go back to her, or so Dominique tells him.

'That can't happen to me, can it?'

'You know it can't, Robert. You know your mother's dead.'

'No, I mean my father.'

'Well, you know . . .'

'Couldn't he change his mind?'

'We don't know who he is, Robert.' They have discussed this before. But she is not surprised that it keeps coming up.

'It couldn't happen to you either, because you're adopted.

We adopted you, because your family couldn't be found. So no one can take you away from us.'

'Yes, but if he's alive, he might know that I am here, that I'm alive, and come to look for me.'

Dominique pauses.

'I doubt it. Frankly.'

'How can you be sure?'

'Your father is not listed on your birth certificate, Robert. Nobody knows who – '

'Well, he still might come.'

Dominique sighs.

'He might, Robert, he might. But I don't think he will. Honestly, that's what I think. I don't think he will ever come.'

The curved wooden banisters, poised and symmetrical, symbolised a calm that contrasted sharply with the noise of traffic outside the library walls. They seemed to welcome her, like two enveloping arms, inviting her to step up the cool white flagstones. The overhead fans in the foyer of the Bibliothèque Bernheim swished already; eight-thirty in the morning and the heat was rising.

Catherine paused. Which way to go, where even to start?

A sign directed her to local history. Here were periodicals, bulletins, gazettes, replicas of authentic documents, maps, books, photos of colonial Nouméa.

New Caledonia. First annexed by the French in 1853 when it was 'feared the British would take possession'. How close to becoming another English colony, she thought, studying the engraving of Captain Cook at the time of his discovery of the island in 1774.

She allowed herself to be sidetracked, attracted to the history of migration and the mix of ethnicities in the developing country. French, English, Irish, Chinese, Indonesian, Japanese, Arab, Indian: all had their stories beside, and not always harmoniously with, the indigenous Kanaks.

Kanak. The Melanesian word for 'man', inhabitants of the islands from the eleventh century, though their ancestors, the Lapita, were thought to have arrived from Vanuatu in about 1500 BC. Originating mostly from Western Polynesia – Samoa, Tonga and Wallis Islands. They were followed by European arrivals during the sixteenth century; the Spanish, English and French. The whalers and the sandalwood traders. The missionaries to the Loyalty Islands, the political prisoners – *les communards* – from the Paris Commune uprising of 1871. *Colonisation.* Century-old hostilities between the Kanaks and the French settlers encroaching on their lands. The revolt of 1878 and the deaths of twelve hundred Kanaks. The *indigénat* code, placing Kanaks outside of French common law. More Indonesians, Tahitians, Japanese, Vietnamese: labour imported to exploit the rich mining resources of the country. The World Wars, the birth of the independence movement, the nickel boom . . .

After two hours of browsing it was time to focus her research. Nagging in the back of her mind was the idea of returning to *Le Journal* to browse the newspaper archives. Hadn't Henri seemed welcoming?

She was not far from his office as she stepped out in the sunlight, but turned and headed back to the bus station.

Tomorrow. She might go tomorrow.

———

They have known each other since kindergarten. Robert has an image of her in the sun, on the verandah of the *maternelle* looking out to sea. At morning tea-time the four-year-olds would be lined up and sat in a row looking out to the grand limestone formations which jutted straight up out of the sea. One rock they called *La Poule*, since it looked like a sitting hen, the needles of rock under the green hilltop resembling its nest of straw. Mademoiselle Pascale would tell them that it was also known as the tower of Notre Dame, like the one in Paris and that they would all visit there one day.

Robert would always scramble to get her hand when they had to walk in twos. The pair would sit together on the raised step, brown knees knocking together. Rosina sang funny songs and made silly faces. He liked her mass of thick springy curls, sometimes he would bounce his hand on them when the *institutrice* wasn't looking. 'Keep your hands to yourself, Robert, people don't like you touching,' she would say if she caught him.

Rosina's family are Tahitian, her father fishes and her mother looks after the eight children in the family. They are the only Tahitian family in the town. Not many other drivers from the mines have moved up the coast.

Later, in elementary school, Robert is invited to their house, back behind the main street of the town. They eat fish cooked on the wood barbeque and listen to Rosina's father on the guitar. It always comes out when the brothers visit, all with their families. The number of people on these occasions is more than Robert can count. The kids are all out on the road, the girls skipping with a huge rope, the boys down at the beach or up behind the town at the river. He is always torn; he likes Rosina's cousins but he prefers her company.

Even then, he could remember wanting her all to himself.

Seven

Tuesday. Today would be a good day to go back to *Le Journal*. The weather was changing, slabs of grey cloud hung oppressively over the town, and the hot wind had a threat in it. Should she walk or take a taxi? She decided to walk, tucking in her umbrella just in case.

As she entered the town the rain started pelting down, catching her before she could even raise the umbrella. The wind was whipping up. Tree bark and old plastic bottles bowled down the street. The palms bent over on a slant, fronds slapping onto trunks.

Catherine leapt across an overflowing gutter and made it to shelter at the bus station. The water was warm, the air around her still heavy with humidity. She pushed back cords of hair from her eyes and looked around, feeling strangely exhilarated. The streets had suddenly emptied, after seeming so busy five minutes ago.

The rain seemed to ease off for a moment before punching down aggressively. The shelter offered little protection. Still, it wasn't far to the office of *Le Journal*.

She splashed along the grey street, watching the few remaining pedestrians huddle under shop awnings.

Catherine hesitated at the entrance to the office. She must look a sight.

She took the stairs, two at a time and pushed open the door. It was the same receptionist at the front desk. Catherine noted her immaculate appearance; petite, forty perhaps, but well preserved, make-up expertly applied. She raised her eyebrows at Catherine, the mix of curiosity and disdain reminding her of Vivi.

'Madame? Can I help you?'

'Oh, I'm sorry, I got caught in the storm.' Catherine smiled. 'I've arranged to meet with Monsieur Boulez sometime to research the archives.'

The smile was not returned.

'He's not in. He's away for a few days.'

'Oh,' said Catherine. 'Is Martine in? He said that I might speak to her.'

'I'm Martine,' said the woman. 'He didn't mention it.'

'He didn't? Well, I only saw him a few days ago. My name is Piron, Catherine Piron.' She extended her hand, as if it might make a difference.

'Yes, I've met you.' Martine paused a moment, deciding whether or not to be helpful. '*Eh bien*, come on then, I'll show you,' she replied finally, declining the handshake. 'Régine! Look after the front desk, will you?'

Catherine followed Martine downstairs, noting the upright carriage, the size eight. Hours at the gym or the beautician, no doubt. Vivi, again.

'Here they are,' said Martine, pushing open the door into a room hardly bigger than a broom cupboard. 'They start in 1971 and go in chronological order until 1993, last year. Help yourself.'

This time Catherine couldn't hide her disappointment. 'Only from 1971?'

Martine looked at her. 'We only started in 1971.'

Clearly Martine was not about to share any insights into the press that predated 1971, and Catherine decided against this line of enquiry. She would find out from Henri later.

'Thank you,' she said, without turning. 'Thank you, you've been so helpful.'

Catherine stood a while looking at the thick green tomes. Where to start?

On impulse she took down the first volume. In 1971 she would have been thirteen and with the sisters in the dismal Parisian convent school. She would look through, anyway.

The book was so heavy she had to sit, squashing herself uncomfortably into a corner. She leafed through the pages, hardly focussing on anything in detail, trying to gain an impression of the times. Nothing jumped out at her, as somehow she imagined it might, no 'news in brief', none of the social or sporting events, though she lingered on headlines about the Pacific Games and the Auckland-Nouméa yacht race. She checked the death notices, paused on the details of plane arrivals and departures, mused on the photos of school children performing a *Pilou* – the Kanak dance. A notice about an irate landlord evicting a tenant for non-payment of the rent caught her attention. Precious little anonymity here. You defaulted and everyone knew about it.

'Pan American Airways to assure Sydney-Nouméa flights . . .' she skipped over the headlines, skimmed the reports. 'Kouaoua mines to open in 1977. Employment prospects, especially for workers disadvantaged by the 1964 closure of Tiébaghi.'

Nothing she could link to the bare sketch of her family history.

At random she selected another tome. 1984. The year after she had visited on the cruise. *Quatre-vingt-quatre*. It had a rhythm to it, perhaps it was a year she should remember. Browsing through, it seemed she really had stumbled upon a dark year of the country's not-too-distant history. Images of fire, violence and destruction: boycotts, riots, roadblocks, home invasions, properties burnt, bomb explosions, shootings. December, 1984. Hienghène. Nine Kanaks in two trucks returning home after a political meeting in the remote north of the island when they were ambushed, massacred, their assassins fleeing into the mountains.

Hooked now, Catherine took down the next volume. Early January, 1985. A young Caledonian boy, seventeen years old, shot by a sniper at his family property. The *indépendantiste* who had held a township to siege, shot by gendarmes. Loyalist riots erupting in Nouméa, protesting the government's handling of the independence conflict: young *lycéens*, teenagers, stoning the vans of the special police, buildings on fire, hand grenades, tear gas, state of emergency. How did it end? Had it ended?

1988. She remembered something now, from the news at home. Three French gendarmes assassinated by Kanak militants on the island of Ouvéa: a siege, hostages held in a cave, the special forces liberating them, resulting in the deaths of nineteen Kanaks and two French soldiers. Isolated attacks throughout the rest of the country, the presidential elections in France, Mitterand returned to power.

Overwhelmed, she closed the book. She had left her watch at the hotel, but knew it must be approaching noon by the rumblings in her stomach. Outside the rain was stopping and starting, but the wind was still strong. She wondered about returning to Didi's restaurant for lunch. Maybe Henri was right. She would have to get to know some of the locals. Here she was fossicking around in the dark. The next step was to go to the *Mairie*, or perhaps to the churches to see if she could look at records. But she needed an entrée, and Henri was her best chance. Perhaps she would ask Martine for another appointment.

'Oh,' said Martine, as if amused that someone should want to organise such a thing. 'I think he is back on Monday. Come back Monday.'

'Could he perhaps ring if he is in before that?' Catherine suggested tentatively. It was suddenly a desolate thought – almost a week without any leads. 'I'll leave you my number at the hotel,' she added, more forcefully. What did she have to lose?

'*D'accord*. Write it here.' Martine pushed a scrap of paper to Catherine, leaving her to dig out a pen from her bag. Then she busied herself at the switchboard. 'We're actually closing up, it's a number one alert.'

'Oh?'

'Cyclone warning. Don't worry.' Her laughter mocked the anxiety on Catherine's face. 'They don't always come to much. You just need to get your washing in and bring in your outside furniture.'

'Oh, all right. Thank you, and I hope to be in again to meet with Monsieur Boulez, *d'accord*?'

Martine shrugged in a non-committal kind of way.

Of course. Catherine thought. *Henri's lover*.

'*Enchantée*.' Catherine extended her hand for the second time.

'*Bonne journée*, Madame,' Martine replied, approximating a handshake.

Catherine left the office, opening the doors to the gales of wind and rain. The taxi rank was further away than the bus station – maybe she would eat first and then call a taxi from the restaurant. On second thoughts, if there was an alert perhaps she was better off to go straight back and have lunch at the hotel. She opened her umbrella to brave the walk to the station.

Arriving, there were few people waiting. She wondered anxiously if the alert had been upgraded.

'Excusez-moi,' she started, to the woman next to her. She saw it was the Melanesian woman from the bus the other day. 'Oh, bonjour, Madame,' she added, as the older woman raised her eyebrows in acknowledgment.

'You should get back home, it's a number one alert,' said the woman. She had a gentle, slow voice that struck Catherine as soothing. 'Cyclone warning,' she repeated, raising her voice through the din of the rain.

'Oh,' said Catherine. 'Is it safe to catch a bus?' she looked around her. Not many cars were on the streets and certainly no taxis.

'My grand-daughter is collecting me in a few minutes. You can have a lift with her if you like.'

She smiled, a polite, almost deferential smile.

'You are at the hotel, yes?'

'Yes, Les Alizés. A lift would be wonderful. You recognise me, don't you, from the other day on the bus?'

The old woman looked into Catherine's face, as if tracing its contours with her eyes.

'Yes,' she said, then seemed to frown. 'Yes, I recognise you . . .'

The conversation was left hanging a little in the air. Catherine wondered if she had offended the older woman somehow. She extended her hand.

'Catherine Piron. Enchantée.'

'Louise.' She smiled, lowering her eyes. A little white Renault pulled up close to the shelter. 'Here is Hélène now.'

Louise ushered Catherine into the front seat, waving away her protests. 'My old legs are shorter than yours!'

Hélène drove slowly down the grey road, leaning forward in an attempt to see more clearly. It was like driving through the sea; the windscreen wipers not up to the task of clearing the water.

They travelled in silence. Once the weather had been covered it was hard to introduce a topic. Catherine hoped she wouldn't have to explain herself and her mission, also sensing a reticence, perhaps borne of politeness, from the two women. Besides, Hélène was concentrating too hard on the driving for polite conversation.

'Thank you again,' Catherine said, descending. 'See you at the bakery soon.'

'If the weather improves,' said Hélène. 'Sometimes everything just shuts down.'

'Ah, Madame Piron,' called the receptionist as she walked in. 'A message for you.'

Surprised, Catherine took the note and unfolded it.

Henri Boulez. 263472.

'Oh, did he say what he wanted?'

'No, Madame.'

Back in her room, she dialled the number quickly. A recorded message announced that, due to the alert, *Le Journal* was closed for the afternoon.

Damn. Why had he given her that number?

She would just have to sit it out.

~⚬~

The little school on the east coast has a fluctuating population, but today there are fourteen eight-year-olds who await Mademoiselle Desarmagnac's programme for the day, the first day of school for the year. It is not complicated: introductions, spelling, *dictée*, reading, maths, physical education. Her job is to get through it, regardless, to see that there are not too many misunderstandings or disagreements, and that she remembers to collect the exercise books at the end of the day.

The class is mainly boys, but there are a few girls whose

eyes seek hers as she enters. One especially takes her attention, a brown-eyed Tahitian girl with thick springy hair and a generous smile; a smile that needs no encouragement. She returns it, thinking the day may turn out well after all. The girl has her hand up and seems keen to speak.

'Mademoiselle,' she says, politely and with confidence. 'Do you have a fiancé?'

Mademoiselle Desarmagnac is taken aback, but then, there is no need to be defensive.

'What is your name?'

'It's Rosina Tamanu.'

'So – a fiancé. Well, yes, I suppose I have, in a way.'

'Where does he live?'

'A long way away. In France actually. Do you know where that is?'

Of course they do, theoretically. It is inculcated from kinder-garten. They have all seen it on the map of the world, the world that most of them will never see.

'Why isn't he here?'

Some of the boys laugh and she wonders if it is at her, though they are looking away. She sees now that one has a comic book open under his desk.

'Well, it just wasn't possible. I accepted the position in this country and he has a job in France. He may come to visit in the summer holidays.' The holidays seem so far away, she thinks. He is so far away.

There is a loud snort of laughter and she turns to the boy she thinks is responsible.

'That's enough, now, there is no need to be disrespectful,' she chides. 'What is your name then?'

'Mademoiselle,' says Rosina before he can answer. 'Robert wouldn't be rude to you. It wasn't him.'

She hears somebody making a 'hussh' sound at Rosina who turns around and glares them to silence. Mademoiselle Desarmagnac is beginning to appreciate the particular dynamics of the class. As far-flung as it is from her home, it is not so unlike it. She turns back to the boy she thought was laughing at her and sees he has lowered his eyes. No, Rosina would be right. He doesn't look like the sort.

'All right class, now we've had introductions, let's get on with some work. Take out your exercise books. We're going to write about what we did in the holidays.'

———◯

The cyclone alert was downgraded. The weather calmed, though it retained the threat and humidity. The hotel room felt claustrophobic; Catherine started to doubt the wisdom of her decision to come. How did she manage at home? Friends, she supposed. Always someone you could ring, someone who would help you get through the low moments.

But would she have shared this story, even if she had had the time before she left? She'd told no one; made up excuses to get the contact for Henri. Was it shock that prevented her, or fear or shame? Ashamed of what might be revealed of the life of her father, whose roots were also hers?

Why had she never pursued his story? Thinking back, it seemed to her that the doors had been slammed shut if ever she raised any questions. You just accepted the bare answers if you were the daughter of a forceful woman such as Marthe. You had no standing, really, a mere child, for whom everyone else judged what was best, about whom decisions were made. What right did you have to information? It had all seemed acceptable to her as a child. She'd just grown up without a father. And now, to think that the door had been so tightly closed on one complete half of her family history, just like that. In being denied the truth of her father's existence she felt her own life had become somehow inauthentic. What *was* her life? Who was she?

There was nobody who would understand she decided, rightly or wrongly, not even her closest friends. It was too painful to raise, not anywhere, not with anyone.

On Saturday night Robert is allowed to come to the dance. The band comes around once every few months, this Saturday it is to their village. Everyone will be there. But he stays outside the hall with the other kids his age; it's too smoky and noisy inside and smells of beer already. They'll go down to the river and pull out the bamboo raft from the reeds. There is enough light by the moon; they'll go over to the other side where they can swing out on the rope over the dark water. It's a long, knotted rope; takes up to nine of them, all hanging together in a clutch. The last one to drop off is the winner. Robert has not won yet; most of the others are ten or eleven, and bigger than he is. The water is warm; he'll dry off easily before they have to go home. He is about to leave when he sees Rosina, framed in yellow at the doorway of the hall. She calls out to them.

'Let me come too!'

'Okay.'

The others don't care – they're stronger anyway and she'll drop off easily.

There are eight of them including Rosina, nearly too many for the raft. It dips under the water line. But they make it over and clamber off onto the bank. Rémy hoists the rope in with a bamboo pole, the others jostle for the best position on the launching stone.

Tonight Robert is feeling strong. Laurent drops off first, laughing as he bombs the water. He wanted a dip anyway, he calls out, spraying silver blades of water as he swims strongly back to the bank. Robert digs Olivier in the ribs, and when he doesn't drop, tickles him with his free hand, his other gripping the rope. He is squashed into the writhing, laughing mass of bodies. Above him, a foot presses down on his head – he hadn't managed to get the highest position. Rosina seems unsure of the game.

'It's okay, hold on to me.'

She clings tightly to him, her arms around his chest, her thin dress wet and flapping against his skin. He has never felt so good.

The tickling is a new strategy, and it seems to work. With one hand he draws a finger-nail down the sole of the foot above him. Somebody's foot is on his shoulder, he shrugs it off. His thighs are sinewy and strong and his feet curl around the knots. His body is flexible, agile, secure; the others all drop like torpedoes until only he and Rosina are left circling in a wide free arc over the moonlit river.

Although he is only nine years old, he feels older at this moment. As if he has a memory of this in another time; a sure knowledge that he is invulnerable. A leader perhaps, since he has won tonight. He likes the idea. If he could, he would swing here all night, Rosina's smooth thighs entwining his own. They would glide together, untouchable, high above them all.

When they return to the dance hall he loses the feeling of safety in an instant. They slow at the guttural sounds of jeering, vaunting, insult. The music is playing half-heartedly inside, stopping and starting; it seems to have lost the beat. It's not the first dance he's been to and he knows how they always end. In the channel of light from the doorway to the hall there are two men fighting; around the side of the hall he can hear the sound of pissing or vomiting. The smell of alcohol assaults his nostrils, unsettles him, reminds him of violence. His eyes widen as he sees the sisters of his friends scuttling back from wherever they have been; in the long grass behind the hall, or leaning on cars. Laughing, or crying, he can't tell which.

The fight is getting serious. He expects Gaëtan to appear at any moment, or Dominique, and scuffle him away. But as he skirts around the scene he recognises one of the men arguing as Jean-Paul, his step-brother.

Robert watches Jean-Paul draw himself back ready to throw a punch at his opponent, a man he doesn't recognise, a Kanak, probably a station hand from another farm. Impulsively he steps into the breach, oblivious to Rosina's calls to prevent him. He doesn't have a chance, though. Someone swoops down on him as he is about to launch himself onto Jean-Paul's sleeve.

'Stop it kid, we're out of here!' It is Gaëtan, and Dominique at his side, her face like turbulent water. 'Where have you been?' she snaps at him.

'Jean-Paul!' he calls, as his brother, momentarily surprised, starts to clench his hands into fists, thrusting his jaw forward. His mouth spits slackly. 'Fumier . . .'

'Leave him, it's not our affair,' says Gaëtan. He bundles up the protesting boy, indicating with a toss of his head to Dominique that it is time they disappeared.

'But – he'll hurt him!' Robert doesn't know what would be worse – if Jean-Paul gets hurt or hurts the man he's fighting. Either way, there'll be trouble.

Gaëtan keeps walking. Some are calling out for the men to stop, others spurring them on. Son or not, Gaëtan is not prepared to insert himself into the fight, has long ago renounced the role of peace-keeper in matters between young men of different creed; whether it be family or land, race or religion. He doesn't know what the fight is about but it will be over soon enough, he thinks, and it will be a lesson to both of them, however it turns out.

Dominique thinks she knows the source of the conflict. Jean-Paul has been seeing the station hand's sister, who still lives in the *tribu*. The girl can't be more than fifteen, if that. She could try to divert it, this fight, for another day, that's as much as she could do. She can at least try.

'Jean-Paul,' she calls out, her voice sounding thin against the jeers. 'Leave it. Fighting will not solve it. It is not the answer.'

Jean-Paul is too old to listen to her entreaties, and not wise enough to know he should. They have both thrown a punch. His lip is thick with the taste of blood and he smells blood on his opponent. But the station hand has drunk more – his gestures are imprecise, the slurs are degrading, becoming meaningless. Gaëtan senses the moment at the same time as some of the other bystanders.

'Yeah, leave it, boys. Let off.'

Gaëtan grabs Jean-Paul by one arm and tries to organise him into a frogmarch. He shakes his father off, but seems willing, finally, to slump onto the shoulder of his little brother.

'*Allez, on y va.*'

They leave the scene, Dominique proclaiming that she is no longer willing to be part of all this, nor will she, not by any persuasion, be attending the next dance.

Eight

Catherine stood up from the bed and walked to the balcony. There must be something else she could do. In a moment she decided to go out again but was stopped by the phone ringing.

'*Allô*, Catherine?'

'Oh, Henri.' Catherine dropped back on the bed, surprised. 'I thought you were away.'

'I had to come back because of the cyclone.'

'Yes, but there isn't one now,' Catherine said pedantically. She felt annoyed with herself. The conversation had got off on the wrong track.

'I know, I know, but I had to come back to secure my yacht.'

'Your yacht?'

'Well, it's actually my *salon* as well, and my kitchen.'

'Oh?'

'It's my home. I had to come back and prepare it for the cyclone if there was to be one. But enough of that. I am here. Anyway, you called in to *Le Journal*?'

'Yes, this morning.' Catherine was still trying to envisage the yacht.

'Listen, the office is closed now but I can open it up for you if you like.'

Catherine paused. She didn't feel like returning to the broom cupboard. Besides, she probably wasn't going to find out much more just by browsing.

'Well . . .'

'What's the matter, you don't sound very enthusiastic. You are strange, you *pokens*. Hot one day, cold the next, hot, cold, hot, cold. Which is it today?'

Piqued, she defended herself.

'I'm sorry, I didn't want to trouble you, and I was a little tired, that's all. I'm not used to this heat. And what is a *poken*, please?'

'Oh, that. A *poken* – English *spoken* here. Australians you know, that's what we call you.'

'But I'm French, remember?'

'*Allez, allez*, I'm too bored with this conversation,' Henri interjected, to Catherine's relief. 'Come to my deck and have a drink with me,' he continued. 'I have brought back fruit from the east coast, *papaye, mangue, banane*, pineapple, passionfruit. I will make you a thick cocktail, come.'

Catherine broke out laughing. His tone was almost affectionate.

'Well, where do I come?'

It was Henri's turn to laugh. 'Ah, you mean, you *do* want to come? You don't worry that you are coming in the storm to a yacht with a strange journalist who may not be trusted?'

'Well . . .'

'Stay there,' said Henri. 'I come for you in ten minutes. Les Alizés, non?'

She was still wavering when she heard the phone click.

Catherine sat staring at the wall after she had replaced the receiver. Had he said ten minutes? That wasn't long enough to get ready, why hadn't she suggested forty-five?

She dashed to the shower, forgetting herself for a moment under the warm spray. *What should she wear for a fruit cocktail on a yacht?*

Dropping her wet towel on the floor, Catherine snatched a sundress from the wardrobe, dressed hurriedly and fled the room, sneaking out the fire escape.

She walked briskly to the street, flagging the first taxi to come into view around the bend.

'To the boulangerie,' she said to the driver, having no other idea where to go.

'Which boulangerie, Madame? There are hundreds.'

'Oh, the one just down here a little further and – left just along here. There it is! How much is that?'

'Five hundred francs,' he answered, his puzzled look telling her he couldn't make out what kind of French she spoke.

She fumbled for coins. 'I'm a *poken*,' she said, in French, just to see his reaction.

'Ah *oui*, but you speak such beautiful French – perfect!'

'I know, I know,' she replied. 'Thank you. I'm sorry it was such a short ride.'

'*De rien*, Madame, it does not matter! A *poken*, eh, who would have thought!'

Catherine scrambled out onto the footpath, trying to straighten her clothing.

It was the afternoon run at the Boulangerie du Boulevard. Catherine could see Hélène in the steamy interior, busily serving the file of customers moving past. Damp and limp, the baguettes drooped over the edges of the wire racks, such was the humidity in the air after the morning rains. In the corner at a small table sat Louise, passing the time of day, watching the shoppers, perhaps waiting for her grand-daughter.

Catherine joined the queue, forgetting her impulsive flight from the hotel. She smiled at Hélène.

'Hello again! I'll try an almond croissant this time. They look irresistible.'

'That or the *millefeuille*, Madame, you should treat yourself, you are on holiday. It looks as if you have been running to work it off!'

'You can see how unfit I am! But please, give me one of those anyway.'

Hélène wrapped the *millefeuille* carefully and handed it to Catherine.

'Three hundred francs, please.'

'I'm not really here on holiday,' Catherine said, collecting her change from the tray.

Hélène raised her eyebrows in curiosity, but turned to the next customer.

'Sorry,' said Catherine. 'You can't talk now, of course. Maybe we could . . .' What could she suggest? She had nowhere to invite them.

'Talk to my grandmother,' said Hélène, as if reading her thoughts.

Catherine approached Louise's table. 'Hello again, Madame,' she started. 'So – no cyclone?'

Louise smiled in response. 'You said you would be here soon,' she pronounced. Her eyes were bright with anticipation, as if she had overheard Catherine's conversation with Hélène.

'I was telling Hélène I'm not exactly here on holiday. I'm doing research of a sort. My family history.'

The older woman seemed to chew this over. 'Your family is here?'

'Not any more. At least – well, my father lived here for a time, in the late fifties.'

'And now?'

'I don't know. Actually, it's possible that he is still here.'

'What is his name?'

As Catherine opened her mouth to speak a car alarm started up outside, drowning her out. The noise filled the bakery.

A commotion of horns followed.

'Ransan,' said Catherine, raising her voice.

'Sorry? I can't hear,' replied Louise, wrinkling her face.

'Ransan, Georges Ransan.'

'I'm sorry,' Louise looked around at the clientele, appealing to someone to manage the situation.

Failing, she clasped Catherine's hand and shook her head.

'Come for tea,' she said. 'Tomorrow. Six rue Paddon, above the bay.'

'Oh, that's kind,' said Catherine.

'For tea,' repeated Louise. 'Come at four o'clock.'

Catherine left the bakery and the disputing motorists, clutching her *millefeuille* in its thin paper wrapping, just managing to keep the cream from staining her dress. You didn't eat *millefeuille* on the run, she thought, recalling Vivi sweeping her in to the Patisserie St Germain – 'Absolutely, *ma cocotte*, there is no other for *millefeuille!*' You sat down and had tea and ate them daintily, you took time, appreciating their subtle vanilla flavour.

Catherine headed in the direction of the beach, ambivalent about returning to her hotel. The wind had dropped, though the skies were still grey.

She'd eat it under the *citronniers*, and probably get sand in it.

It is eleven o'clock on Sunday morning, a beautiful Parisian autumn day, still slightly crisp. Outside the sun shines cold and bright through the branches of the trees now losing their leaves, the trees along the river leading away from the convent. The others are changing their clothes after mass, soon they'll be called to set the table for lunch. I hear the knock at the door and the kind wife exclaiming what a beautiful day it is for a walk in the gardens, such a beautiful day.

Last Sunday I went the same way with Monsieur Girard and his wife. I can picture it exactly: the park where the rows of triangular shrubs lead through to a garden of statues and a maze. I followed the concentric circles of the maze, going around and around until I felt so dizzy I fell to the ground. I stayed there, loving the dizziness and the way the sky reverberated blue and hazy, scrunching my eyes against the white glare of the statues. I lay motionless, until Monsieur Girard must have realised that his charge had disappeared, and had come hurrying over.

'Catherine, *ma petite*, are you all right?'

'Of course, Monsieur, I was only pretending.'

'You are hurt? You fell?'

'Of course not. I'm looking at the sky.'

Puzzled, Monsieur Girard had glanced up, as if to gaze at the sky might unravel a wondrous, untold mystery. He had smiled at me, in any case.

'It is time to go now, Catherine.'

Time to go? I could not believe my ears. Was I now to return to the convent? Was this not the beginning of forever, this outing with the kind stranger and his wife, whose origins and identity were a mystery to me, but who had appeared for some heaven-sent reason, supposedly an acquaintance of my mother, to take me one Sunday to the gardens I would later discover were none other than the gardens of the Palace of Versailles.

I overhear the exchange of greetings, hear Monsieur Girard and his wife being asked to take a seat.

'It is very curious,' I hear, 'but we are afraid, *la petite* seems to have gone missing. She was certainly here at breakfast, we saw her with her bowl of hot chocolate. For some reason, most embarrassing for us, Monsieur and Madame, we can't find her; we think perhaps she must be playing some game of hide and seek. Most terribly sorry, Monsieur, to have troubled you and your wife; she was to have reported to the foyer at five minutes to eleven. So very sorry to waste your time, especially as she was so very happy after the last visit. Perhaps next Sunday? Please don't hesitate, I hope this has not daunted you.'

But I know, as I listen through the thick oak panel of the closet in the foyer, where I have hidden myself after mass and where they will eventually find me after dinner that evening; after, finally, the police have been called — after, almost, they talk of contacting my mother — I know there will be no more outings on Sunday.

After the turn-off they continue along a back road, cutting through an avenue of shady trees: palms and mango-trees, huge banyans tangled with bougainvillea. Robert is pleased that he can remember the way, that *he* can show *her*, even though she walks a little in front. Rosina picks frangipani flowers as she goes, tucks a hibiscus flower behind her ear. The black teeth of the basalt cliffs crouch above them on the riverside of the road. Robert feels as if they are inside a hatching egg, looking up at black lace turned to stone, and beyond that the already deep blue sky glazed by the morning heat.

There are fewer cars along this road; they pass a woman returning from the village laden with shopping, an old rusted truck growing into the grass, two kids on bikes. Every now and again little pathways detour off the road, in the breaks between the trees, leading to houses, rough concrete dwellings with bark roofs, or cleared blocks of land, through which they catch a glimpse of the sea. From this distance it appears large and unmoving, calm and watchful.

Meeting the river they wade across, for there is no bridge and to turn back inland will only waste time. The water is only momentarily fresh on their skins, the day has already warmed. They wade thigh deep until they reach a faster-flowing channel in the middle. Robert smiles as Rosina breaks into laughter, suddenly neck deep in the water and bowled along by the current, her dress billowing up beneath her.

'Hey! Catch me!'

He jumps out, trapping her fingers, feeling for a moment that his strength is preventing her from flowing away, though he knows she can keep herself afloat. It is not too wide here at the river mouth, less than ten metres; she will make it across easily. Her hair floats out like a tiara, like a halo, and when she shakes her head, the white droplets spin on the water.

They scramble through the mangrove roots on the other side of the river and pick up the road again, passing some trees she tells him are called *folie de jeune fille*, showering their pink flowers over the road. This time they accept a lift a few hundred metres along. Just enough space for them in the back of the pick-up, between the bony dogs, cans of kerosene, coils of rope, fishing tackle.

'Where are you off to so early?' asks the driver.

'Tao. *La cascade.*'

'Skipping school?'

To this Robert shrugs, and the rest will be left unsaid. He has predicted, rightly, that the conversation will come to a natural end at this point.

The driver pulls up outside a rudimentary concrete house, just visible behind the clumps of banana trees. He jerks a thumb at a hand-painted sign indicating that visitors should pay 100 francs to the owners for the privilege of bathing at the falls, 'children less than twelve years, free'.

'You should just get by, I'd say.'

The track is flat for about three hundred metres, then rises sharply. They can no longer hear one another for the roar of the water, suddenly louder as they come through a sheltered thicket of ironwoods. Even the birdsong, so shrill till now, seems to have ceased. Below them are the tops of tree ferns; shady umbrellas fanning over the path; above, to the left they have a partial view of the cascade, a milky-white streak against the backdrop of black rock and luxuriant green. In the foreground, a kaleidoscope of rock pools, smashed like cut glass in the sun, stretching back in a million shattered mirror-images to the concealed base of the falls.

There she is above him, sure as a mountain goat, climbing higher and higher, springing from slimy boulder to boulder, never slipping. At one point he loses sight of her, a grey outcrop blocking his view.

At eleven he is more modest than she. Her dress is still damp from the river, so it is not for want of keeping it dry that she removes it. Tossing it behind her, she tests the depth of the closest pool with one foot. He hangs back, suddenly overawed. She seems to have forgotten his presence, off to one side, partly in shadows. No other sound can be heard above the noise of the water, and he realises that, anyway, it would be unlike her to shout at him.

Dipping his foot into the rapids, he feels it cool on his toes. He is distracted by her honey skin, her partially clad body. Does he dare sneak a longer look? To take off his shirt is not as significant as for her to have taken off her dress. His thoughts stray to the boys in class, at this moment opening their exercise books for *dictée*. There is *no way* he will drop *his* shorts, let alone underclothes, even as now, she emerges completely naked from the pool, without so much as a glance in his direction.

And yet to remain clothed seems suddenly so at odds with the scene before him. He'll join her, he decides. His first step away from childhood, just as nakedness, for her, is its last vestige.

'Hey!' she turns to him, finally raising her voice over the roar. 'We can slide down here!'

He is more cautious. How easy it would be to fall, to break your neck even.

'I'll go first – you watch,' he says.

Even before he is able to test the safety of the boulder-slide, the force of the current bats him over, his feet slipping on the moss, his body following like a bag of potatoes. Going under he hears her voice like a bird-cry from above – she could do nothing to help, if he'd been pushed too far. He manages to catch onto a fallen log, placed, it seems, for his convenience. He rises up in a float, face down, legs splayed out horizontally, just to the side of a whirlpool.

'It's okay here – I'll catch you if you miss the tree!' he calls.

She is scrambling towards him, letting her body skitter over the rocks, missing the log in a flounder of arms and hair. Anxious for a second, he scoops the water to find her, but she torpedoes up, like a brilliant genie from a bottle. As he reaches for her hand, all sound still drowned, he can see only bold evidence of laughter across her face, her wide, joyous mouth and her exultant eyes.

A smile he will see again and again in dreams and know that it will survive.

⎯⎯◯

Catherine lingered at the reception desk as the clerk passed over her room key.

No, no messages for Madame.

She flinched inwardly, imagining Henri enquiring. *But she was here just a few minutes ago, I spoke to her on the phone. This is bizarre.*

The staff were changing shift. Catherine recognised the reception clerk from the previous evening.

'*Excusez-moi*, Madame,' he said.

'Yes?'

'Madame Piron, *n'est-ce pas?*'

'Yes, that's me.'

'A man called for you this afternoon, Madame, but you were out.'

'Oh?'

'A Monsieur Boulez, from *Le Journal*.'

'Did he . . .' started Catherine, hoping she didn't look flushed. 'Did he leave a message?'

'No, he didn't.'

She sensed the clerk waiting for her to look at him directly. He had a sympathetic air, and she felt suddenly vulnerable.

'But he said – to himself that is, he said: *C'est pas grave*. It doesn't matter. That's what he said.'

'Oh, well – thank you,' said Catherine.

'Good afternoon, or, almost good evening to you, Madame.'

'Yes, you too – Emmanuel, *n'est-ce pas?*'

'*C'est exact*, Madame.' Emmanuel inclined his head politely.

Catherine walked towards the stairs, then paused. *C'est pas grave*. It doesn't matter. Did he mean it didn't *matter* that she had run out on him – or that he forgave her?

She turned and walked back out of the hotel onto the promenade, stuffing her room key into her bag and thinking that her sandals clacked too much.

She kept walking, straight ahead would do. She didn't have the first idea where she was going.

The sugar had dissolved in her coffee, but Catherine kept stirring. Marthe's eyes, taking over the space between the lines of sea and sky. Marthe is dead. Buried or cremated? Did she care?

'Something else, Madame?' said the waiter, startling her.

'What, oh no, sorry.'

'The bill perhaps?'

'Yes, just the bill, it's late, isn't it?'

'Yes, Madame.'

Everything was closing up.

The waiter watched her leave, a strange, solitary soul. Like a bird bobbing across an empty beach, too late for the crumbs.

Nine

Louise's house was up on the hill, overlooking the Baie de l'Orphelinat. Catherine had decided to walk. The hill was steep and she had to keep stopping to take a breath. At least it meant she could catch the broadening view of the sunlit bay. The afternoon sun was dipping, streaking filaments of gold across the sea. A group of catamarans was coming in, perhaps students on a sailing lesson. The boats cut smoothly through the glassy water, the sails hardly flapping.

Six rue Paddon. The house was small, dating from the turn of the century, a little cottage with a single band of rusting iron fretwork lining the verandah roof.

Catherine stepped past the wicker rocking chair and the pots of bright red impatiens and tapped at the door. Louise must have been waiting. In an instant it opened before her.

'Bonjour, Catherine, come in, come in.'

The table was set with a teapot and three cups.

'Hélène will come after her shift. She finishes early today.'

Louise moved slowly, pouring the tea, checking requirements for milk or sugar. She's timeless, thought Catherine. She has time and she takes time.

Louise said few words, waiting until the tea was poured and both women were settled. Catherine smiled, recognising a plate of SAO biscuits. They seemed so distinctively Australian, vestiges of a past generation.

'Here, try some jam. Mango, this one. Guava, there, or banana.'

'Do you make them all?' Catherine couldn't help sniffing the pot. 'Mmm – smell the vanilla! Do you grow it here?'

'My family in Tahiti. They always bring some when they come to Nouméa.'

Catherine nodded, her mouth full of biscuit. The smell of vanilla filled the room. 'My mother kept vanilla in her sugar. She must have picked up the habit here.'

Louise nodded. 'I knew a French family once,' she said. 'I was their housekeeper. The mother was so unhappy here she left, taking her little girls.'

Catherine felt the biscuit catch in her throat. She felt dizzily, bizarrely, in another realm, on a precipice or watching herself in a film.

'Are you all right?' said Louise, meeting her eyes.

'You *know* me,' Catherine said, trying to clear her throat. 'Louise, you seem to know me.'

'Wait here a moment.' Louise rose, shuffling slowly from the front room. It seemed like hours before she returned.

'Look at this,' she said, handing her a crumpled, yellow piece of newspaper. Catherine unfolded it, reading aloud. The *Sydney Morning Herald*, 18 January, 1976. She drew in her breath, taking in the story headline, the photo.

'I remember this article. Where did you find this, Louise?' Catherine's hands shook as she tried to focus on the smaller print.

'It was left behind,' said Louise, quietly. 'In a flat that I had to clean up.'

'My father,' said Catherine. 'You knew my father? Georges!'

'Monsieur Georges, that was him, yes. And it's you, isn't it, the photo?'

'You were his housekeeper – our housekeeper.'

'I thought I knew after I saw you the other day, but I wasn't completely sure. You were my little chocolate thief!'

Catherine read aloud from the cutting: '"Catherine Piron, 18, from Buckinghamshire, United Kingdom. One of a growing number of young women from abroad coming to our shores as nannies. Known as 'au pairs' in the long-standing European tradition, these women are seeking to combine adventure with further study. Catherine, originally from France, says her world opened up after a chance encounter led to an opportunity for a passage to Sydney, a new family and a new life in Australia."

'How did he have this? Where . . .' Catherine stopped, overwhelmed, wanting all the information at once, trying to fathom what it meant, for the past, present and future. The jigsaw pieces didn't fit, there were jagged edges where there should have been smooth.

She could see that Louise was moved, troubled by her own questions, yet waiting for Catherine to formulate hers first.

'Is he alive, do you know that, do you know where he is?'

Louise shook her head. 'I don't know where he is. I looked after him when he was on his own after you had left. And then later, again. He came and went a bit.'

Catherine hung on her words.

'He had to leave the flat, you see, he didn't have the rent.'

Was she ready to hear more? To find out about trouble, or what kind of trouble? Perhaps Louise was trying to be kind, the way she put it. She bit her lip on her questions.

'He went up the coast, to the mines at Tiébaghi, the Thunder Mountain. He wasn't afraid of hard work, Georges. He went to Australia, too.'

'Australia!'

'But came back here, I bumped into him again, oh, must have been the seventies. After that I lost touch. You see, I can't read. The last I heard, he was with the mine at Poro.'

So many questions. Not a first or a second or a last question, they were all equally important. Why did he leave us? Why did he stay here? How did he find the article? Do you know, Louise, she wanted to say, I thought he was dead. My mother pretended that he was dead. She only told me a month ago, before she died.

But she said nothing.

Louise looked into her eyes, the sadness large and dark.

'He was not a bad man, your father. He was not bad. But he liked, you know, the horses and then later – those machines.'

A gambler. Catherine flipped the idea around in her head, examined it from a few different angles. A gambler.

They heard footsteps outside and the door squeaked open. It was Hélène.

'Bonjour, Catherine.'

'Hélène, it is her,' said Louise.

'The chocolate thief?' Hélène moved to Catherine and embraced her; a natural, sisterly embrace.

'There is so much to tell,' said Louise. 'And so much to find out.'

'It will have to wait,' said Catherine. She wanted, suddenly, to be alone. 'I think I should go now, and come back again to see you.'

She stood to go. Louise nodded, and Catherine could tell she understood, understood it all.

Her face is shining as she opens her arms to me. I run and sink into the spongy warm skin. She smells different to me, different to my mother, like coconut or sweet soap. Her brown cheeks

are like cushions; I like to squash my own into them. At this
she laughs and I see she has no front teeth. She throws her
head back, then brings it back close to mine. This time it is her
nose, her flat broad nose that is squashed. She holds me back
and looks into my eyes.

'You rascal, you scallywag! Give me back my chocolate!'
Then she feigns a sad smile and her eyes droop. Her eyes are
like the chocolate I have stolen.

I press my fingers into her crinkly black hair. It too is spongy
and thick. I trace my fingers down her face.

'Your eyes are slanty,' I say.

'That's enough.' My mother is suddenly in the room. 'Leave
poor Louise alone. She has work to do.'

We look at each other in silence for a moment, suppressing
our giggles, waiting for my mother to leave the house.

Louise chuckles and pokes me in the stomach. 'You stole my
chocolate. I'll tickle you till you give it back!'

And she tickles and I squeal and in the end she takes the
chocolate, only to return it straight back to me.

Tante Lucie hardly ever speaks, but she makes crackers for
everyone in the afternoon, crisp SAO biscuits with Australian
butter from a tin. She moves slowly and wordlessly through her
business at the farmhouse, indicating with a lift of her eyebrows
that tea is ready, or chuckling quietly, covering her mouth, eyes
averted, when Robert wants more. When she has finished eating
she moves slowly back to her seat by the wood stove and lights
up her pipe. The smoke settles into the creases of her brown
face. She sits and watches and waits. It doesn't seem to matter,
in the life of the rest of the household, that she does not wait

for anything in particular. Tante Lucie waits only for the rhythms of her day, of her life.

Tante Lucie is married, or so it is thought, to old Oukanou, Gaëtan's station hand. Nobody would think to ask where Oukanou and Lucie are from or how long they have been on the farm. They are just there, the two of them, an old couple, like pepper and salt shakers or a pair of darned socks.

'Tante Lucie,' Robert asks one day. 'Who is older? You or Oukanou?'

Tante Lucie just smiles. He wonders if she knows.

Sometimes Tante Lucie brushes her hair in the outhouse where they wash the clothes. Robert tries to sneak a look, curious as to how she manages to get her brush through what looks like an impenetrable hedge of hair. It takes several hard strokes to pierce the wiry grey coils. Puffed up with air they fan even wider around Tante Lucie's face, so that she looks like an enormous hot air balloon about to take off.

Half-asleep in the early morning, Robert hears Tante Lucie moving about before anyone else rises. She will be busying herself with the kettle and the wood fire. When the sun comes up he hears the creak of the back door and the chickens complaining. He imagines her out on her hard bare feet, wide and grained like old wood paddles, off to her *tarodière*, her own small taro terrace, where she will break the earth and watch the water flow down the levels. Or cleaving the taro leaves, those needed to wrap the fish for lunch.

She stands in the earth, she belongs to it.

Sometimes he follows her. She doesn't need help but she doesn't mind him watching.

Tante Lucie works her *tarodière* in the morning, and by nine it is done. At nine, as at four, she prepares the crackers, chipping away at the butter from the green tin, or she'll stir the soup, or iron the clothes with her old black iron. By midday, lunch over, Tante Lucie disappears for three or four hours, then re-emerges from her siesta to take up her place by the stove.

It is a shock for him one day to find her absent.

'Tante Lucie?' he whispers to Dominique. 'She hasn't died has she?'

'Lucie? No, but there's been a death in her *tribu*. She's gone to the ceremonies.'

'Oh. So she has a family? Apart from us?'

'She has a big family. Nine or ten children, I think, all grown up.'

'That many? But where are they now?'

'All over.'

'So where is her *tribu*?'

'Down the coast. They – she and Oukanou – came here a long time ago.'

'Can we visit one day?'

'Well . . .'

'But can we?'

'Perhaps.'

Satisfied or not, the subject is dropped. When Tante Lucie returns, a week later, to her chair by the wood stove, Robert feels comforted. It is like the return of a fixture, a familiar piece of furniture, unreasonably wrenched away, now restored.

Ten

Thursday morning, Henri's office. Catherine had made it past Martine.

'I'm sorry, Henri, I just wanted to apologise for my . . .'

'Your desertion?'

'You could say that. I'm sorry.'

'It is no matter. Forget it.'

'If I could just explain – '

Henri waved her on. 'But I am not interested to hear anything. Now. Listen. I have an idea for you. I have to go to the region of Canala to research a story. It is on the east coast. Why don't you come? You are doing nothing here in Nouméa, why not take the air?'

Catherine said nothing, not sure she could believe what he was saying.

'It is an opportunity. You can talk to people. We'll go to the mining country. Someone will know something. Come. You will come, yes?'

'The mining country? We could?'

'Yes. Will you come?'

'It would be fantastic, Henri, I'd love to come. I have news as well.'

'Save it for the car trip. I am leaving in the morning. I will come by and get you, *d'accord*? This time you will be there?' He winked.

Catherine reddened. 'Sure, what time?'

'Seven, we want to get an early start.'

'How long for? Where will we stay?'

Henri waved away her concerns. 'A few days. I know a place to stay, it is okay, they know me there, *ne te casse pas la tête.*'

'Don't break my head?'

'You know what I mean. Don't worry. I'll take care of it.'

'Henri, would you mind if we passed by a friend's in the morning? She lives not far.'

'Sure, sure. Just be ready.'

Leaving his office Catherine felt a familiar jumpy feeling in her chest. A trip *en brousse* – what luck! And yet – was she crazy, setting off with a man she hardly knew, in a foreign country whose customs she had hardly begun to understand? She tried to counsel herself; what would friends advise? Go, of course, she should go.

How safe it was back home. She'd worked herself into a little groove of comfort; a small, predictable, not-unpleasant life, enough friends, a half-interesting job. Of course, if she faced up to it, she knew it was a life lacking in – well, spontaneity for a start. And emotional connection – not for the first time she felt the acute twinge that always came when she acknowledged that she had no family, no one who was really close.

And now this Henri was offering her a chance to accompany him on a journey into the wild unknown.

Of course she should go. Of course she would.

Henri arrived in a white Peugeot with *Le Journal* printed on the side. Catherine felt hot under Emmanuel's raised eyebrows at the desk.

'You're sure you can keep my luggage for a few days then?'

'No problem, Madame.' The corners of his mouth turned up a little, in a kind of smirk. Catherine had to smirk herself. They did try to be discreet, but she sensed it was not in their nature. As soon as she walked out she knew the story would do the rounds of the hotel.

It was early. Had she eaten, asked Henri. No, no time.

'*En route,*' he said. He seemed impatient. 'Come. Let's move.'

They detoured via Louise's little cottage. Henri left the engine running while Catherine jumped out.

Hélène appeared at the door. '*Mémé* isn't well,' she said. 'I'm not working today.'

'Oh, what is it?' said Catherine, suddenly imagining the worst. 'Can I help?'

'No, no, it's just her blood pressure. It gets a bit high and she should take it easy.'

Catherine stood at the doorway, in a crisis of indecision.

'Are you sure she'll be all right? I have to go away for a few days and I wanted to see her.' She bit her lip. It sounded so self-interested.

'She's fine. You go.'

Still Catherine stood in the doorway. She heard shuffling footsteps behind and Louise appeared, a bathrobe hastily wrapped around. Her face looked greyish and haggard.

'Are you all right?' Catherine embraced her: a *bise* on each cheek. 'I have an opportunity to go to the east coast with Henri from *Le Journal*, you know?'

'Go to Poro,' said Louise. 'That is the last place I know of that he worked.'

'Will you be all right?'

'Of course, of course.'

'She forgets her tablets,' said Hélène. 'She's naughty.' She dug her grandmother in the ribs and Catherine was relieved to see Louise smile.

'Go,' said Louise, pushing her. 'We'll talk when you return.'

Henri's car was chugging over. Catherine embraced Louise again. 'Take care.'

They drove out past the port, past the factories of the industrial quarter, past the toll booths of the *péage*. Henri told her a little about his assignment and then settled into a preoccupied silence. The main highway rolled out before them; they passed housing lots, banana trees sliding down the banks, some edge-of-town shanties. Catherine wasn't sure if impatience was just a part of Henri's manner, or whether she had annoyed him by delaying their departure. In any case, she was content not to have to talk. She wanted to take in the view unfolding before her.

Eventually Henri seemed to emerge from his reflection.

'So – this is not your first time here in Nouméa, I don't think? I mean, apart from as a young child?'

'I visited again in my twenties, in 1983 I think it was. I came on a cruise and I was very seasick. I hated it. I felt so ill and we only had the afternoon to spend in those expensive boutiques with their cranked-up tourist prices. Oh, and I remember the aquarium too, only because I nearly got caught up in a fracas with a group of school students.'

'Well, 1983, that was just before *les événements*,' said Henri. 'Tourism was down around then. Tensions were pretty high.'

'What do you mean, *les événements*?'

'"Political events",' answered Henri. 'When things turned violent.'

'But what was it about? I mean, I know a little.'

'You probably know nothing.'

And you would probably be right, Catherine conceded, slighted nonetheless by his tone. 'I wasn't aware of any political trouble at the time,' she continued. 'I only read about things later in the papers.'

'Like many of your compatriot Australians. And the French for that matter.'

'Well, tell me.'

Henri hesitated. 'You had to be here to appreciate the complexities of the situation. It was, and still is, about land, independence from France, Kanak rights, French pride, *bleu, blanc, rouge*, all that. People died, on both sides, in the name of politics.' He stopped. 'Do you remember anything from your childhood?'

Catherine was silent for a moment, annoyed that he had so quickly changed the topic.

'I was curious, I suppose,' she said finally, 'about the place I had spent the first years of my life. But no, I can't remember anything.'

'Nothing at all?'

'I was only three or four years old.'

'A few flashes, perhaps?'

Catherine looked out to the knuckles of the mountains looming ahead. Blue, purplish blue almost, in the distance.

'The colours, maybe. The blues, the greens. The red flowers of the *flamboyants*. Sometimes I feel I have been here before.' She paused. 'As it happens . . . I've met someone I remember – someone who knew my father.'

'Oh?'

She glanced at him. Even side-on, his eyebrows were rising. '*Vraiment*? Who?'

'Her name's Louise. She's a Melanesian woman, though she

looks as though she might have some Vietnamese or Chinese heritage.'

'Quite possible.'

'She used to housekeep for us. She remembers me.'

'How did you meet her?'

'Just by chance. Her grand-daughter works at the bakery and I kept bumping into them. Louise recognised me from a newspaper cutting she found in my father's belongings. From an Australian paper, one of those feature articles on being an au pair in Sydney. Isn't that incredible?'

'Perhaps for you, but not for here,' said Henri. 'It is a small place. I told you the locals would know something. People can pick out a *poken* from the crowd, they are curious, they ask questions if you come close.'

Catherine smiled at his use of the term.

'If I'm a *poken*, what are *you*? You're not a *caldoche*. You weren't born here.'

'Some people call me *le z'oreille*. It means "ears". I think it's originally from the short haircuts of the *militaires*, the guys doing national service from France. They had crew cuts that made their ears stick out. But anyway, I'm not a *z'oreille*. I was born in Algeria. That makes me a *pied noir*.'

'The same as my father. He must have been a *pied noir* too then. "Black foot". Such a strange term.'

'Your father too? I thought he was Parisian.'

'No, my mother was. They met in Paris. At least I think. I'm not sure of anything now.'

'So, he was a *pied noir* too,' said Henri. 'I think it's pejorative, though the *pied noirs* here define themselves proudly. All I know is, I don't quite have the status of either a *z'oreille* or a *caldoche*.

A pause. In the exchange the significance of Louise's revelations seemed to have been lost.

'I'm not completely accepted as a local,' continued Henri, 'though I've been here for twenty years. Perhaps you could say I'm unique.' He took his eyes off the road to glance at her quickly.

'Why are you being so nice to me?' Catherine dared. 'And after I stood you up too. Why this generosity – your time, everything?'

He didn't answer immediately.

'Perhaps because we share something,' he said eventually. His voice had a gravity to it. Gone was the jocularity, the over-confidence. 'We're both from all over the place.'

'That's true.'

'So we belong everywhere and nowhere, if you like.'

Catherine nodded, stuck for words, a little unnerved by the intimacy of his observation.

They sank back into silence, churning up the road.

The aquarium has a modest entrance and the desk is unattended. I step in, drawn into the museum-like silence. There appear to be no other tourists – perhaps they are all at the beach or shopping. A handwritten sign advertises the entry prices. From another area I can hear the jostling sound of people approaching; jeering voices becoming louder, a few sharp shouts. In the entrance area, obscuring the little glass screens of coloured fish, a group of school students appears. All boys, probably aged about thirteen or fourteen. They don't wear uniforms and I wonder at first if they really are students and, more to the point, whether they are being supervised. It is obviously a bad time to have chosen to visit. I can't help noticing that they don't look Melanesian; they seem bigger, broader, Polynesian perhaps, like Maoris. Not all of them; there are a few whiter faces. I feel self-conscious, as if I stand out.

The boys are too noisy for the calm of the dark interior and I want to boss them into respectful silence. Then I become aware that the jostling appears to be directed at one boy in particular, the shoving and pushing something more than just adolescent group movement.

'*Ta gueule,*' I hear and recognise the ugly slang of expletive.

This boy – the victim – appears smaller than his assailants, as far as I can make out. His skin is lightly tanned; I guess he is of mixed race, a *métis*, not purely one or the other like the rest of the group. I catch his eyes; they are dark and have a look of persecution. Maybe it is not the first time he has been attacked. The bigger boy is threatening without yet touching him; he seems to have the swell of the crowd backing him, and I sense the younger boy's fear. As the boys move, some of them brush too close to me and I lose my balance. The bully grabs the younger boy by the arm and begins to twist it, the others jeering on.

'Excuse me, are you with a teacher or something? I'd appreciate being able to look at the displays in silence,' I say loudly, the volume of my voice surprising me. I wonder, too late, at the folly of this, in such an apparently unsupervised zone. I draw in my breath.

Somehow, my authority seems to have the desired effect. It is as if the entire group becomes aware for the first time that there is an outsider in their midst. For all his bluster and swagger, the bully seems to accept the reprimand, and lowers his eyes.

'Pardon, Madame, we were just fooling around.'

'What's going on?' I hear the voice of their teacher finally, as he comes into the area. He is neat, slight, with little round-framed glasses, the complete antithesis to his students. When he speaks I recognise his accent as pure Parisian. 'Are you young people behaving? I'm sorry, Madame,' he says as he catches my flustered look.

'Monsieur, I think they were picking on this young man,' I blurt out.

The teacher looks at the young boy, questioning.

'Are you all right? What was happening?'

'Nothing, nothing,' the boy answers, embarrassed.

'It was nothing, Monsieur,' the other boys say in chorus, 'We weren't picking on him.'

I want to disappear, dissolve, let them sort out the fracas.

'It's time to go, anyway,' says the teacher, 'I'm very sorry, Madame,' he repeats. 'It is the first time for some of them in Nouméa, you see.'

'You're from the country?' I say, glad of the opportunity to change the subject.

'From up the coast, yes. From Bourail, on the west coast, the technical school. Have you visited there? I can see you are not from here.'

'No, no,' I say, thinking how well he has picked my accent. It is certainly not perfectly Parisian.

'You should visit,' he says. 'Too many tourists never see any of the real country. Anyway, apologies again, I wish you a good day.'

As they depart, demurely, a model of perfect behaviour, I watch the boy I had wanted to protect. He walks, a little apart, to the side of the group, shirt untucked, shoulders slumped. He is the last to board the bus. Just before the door closes he turns back, casting his glance at the entrance of the aquarium, as if he knows I am watching.

─────◞

'Jump,' says Gaëtan. He fixes the bamboo pole, balanced on two fence posts, up one more nail.

'Jump, it's only a bit higher.'

Robert takes a few more steps back. He turns, gets into sprint position. He focuses, then drops his head.

'No, it's too high.'

'*Fiston!* It's only a centimetre above the last one. You did the last one. You can do it!'

The boy slumps his shoulders, shakes his body.

'No, I can't.'

'What do you mean you can't?'

'I'll knock it.'

'So you knock it. So it falls off. *Et alors?*'

'I want to leave it at the height I can do, that I know I can do.'

'How do you know you can't do it a centimetre higher?'

'I'm sure I can't.'

'But *how* do you know? You didn't think you could do the last one until you tried. You don't know until you try.'

'I just know I won't be able to.'

Gaëtan taps his forehead, lifts his hands to the sky.

'You can be tough, you can. Tough about what you don't know you're capable of. Why don't you be tough about trying?'

Robert shakes his head.

'I want to leave it now. I'll try again tomorrow.'

Gaëtan looks him in the eye now. He nods slowly, as if finally he understands.

'You'll try tomorrow?'

'I'll try tomorrow.'

Eleven

They stopped at a small café in Boulouparis for breakfast. Henri dipped his croissant in his bowl of café au lait and spoke between mouthfuls.

'We'll turn inland soon,' he said, 'after La Foa. We go up high, through the old coffee plantations.'

'Do we cut through to the other side of the island?'

'Yes, it goes through to Canala, which is near where I have my interview.'

But at La Foa Henri suddenly made a turn, as if he had changed his mind.

'I know a good place for lunch.'

'Lunch? But it's only ten o'clock.'

'We plan early for lunch here.'

As they ascended the steep road the vegetation transformed. Everything was becoming greener, denser, more lush. The mist clung to the lower slopes, and suddenly they were above it, looking down on the thin spires of the colonial pines dotted here and there, splashes of red poinciana blooms, groves of coconut palms and, rising up, a decorated roof spire of a *case*, the traditional thatched habitations, so commonly seen on tourist brochures but here seeming so isolated from that realm.

'Does anyone else come this way?'

'There has been trouble here. Not many tourists come.'

They passed a school, watched gaggles of children out for a break. The colour of the girls' mission dresses brightened the greying backdrop of sky. It looked as if it was about to pour.

'It's too bad, you might have liked to sit by the pool in the rainforest escape. You'll have to come back now.'

They stopped at the *gîte* anyway, in time for an early lunch. Catherine was heady with the exoticism of being escorted into a new landscape. They sat under cover looking out to the pool, the only guests apart from two German tourists.

'What about you, then?' Catherine asked. 'How long did you say you have lived in Nouméa on your yacht?' An image of Martine came irritatingly to mind. Suddenly she was curious. Had he ever been married, did he have children? Probably all grown up if he did.

'Twenty years, thereabouts.'

'Twenty years on a yacht!'

'Well, not all of that time on the yacht.'

Catherine made a quick calculation of his age. Late forties maybe. Perhaps fifty. He looked pretty fit in any case.

'Do you have a photo of your father?' asked Henri.

She hesitated. Nobody else had seen this.

'Just one. It was in the box of stuff my mother kept. We never had any around us growing up, so I'm just getting used to his face.'

Henri took the photo carefully, as if it were a disintegrating piece of lace, and peered at it.

'When do you think this was taken?'

'I guess 1959 or 1960, just after I was born. Apparently he worked on the mines here, at the Thunder Mountain, Louise said.'

'Tiébaghi? But that is closed now. It's a ghost town there.'

'Louise told me he went to Australia too, which is – ironic – I suppose, since I was there too.'

'Where in Australia?'

'I haven't had a chance to ask Louise yet. She mentioned he worked at the mine in Poro too. Are we anywhere near there?'

'It's hard to get through, except by a disgusting road or by boat, from Canala.'

Catherine looked across to the pool, acutely conscious of being at the mercy of his plans. The country seemed suddenly a wilderness, untrammelled, probably magnificently unspoilt in its interior, if ever you could penetrate into its lost valleys and gorges. Hard to get around if you knew no one.

'Is it safe around here, say, if I was on my own?'

'Safe? For you? Not so long ago, I wouldn't have said yes. For example, we pass through Canala. Ten years ago, in 1984, the town nearby, Thio, was under siege and a militant *indépendantiste* was shot by gendarmes. Just six years ago again the country was thrown into upheaval before the presidential elections in France. It was not safe to go to isolated places, not even as a tourist. Since then, well, things have settled a little. You still have to know the people, the customs, and that is hard for a foreigner.'

Catherine prickled at being called a foreigner.

'Tell me more about what is happening on the independence issue?' she ventured, trying again. Henri was right, she felt shamefully uninformed.

'There are still tensions,' he replied. 'It is very complex. We are moving towards a consensus of sorts. There is still a long way to go.'

'What do *you* think? You're a journalist – you write about these things.'

'Ah, yes but I am something of a double agent,' Henri replied mysteriously. 'I do not always agree with what I write, you see. I have my job, yes, but I also have my – personal ideas.' He signalled for the bill.

Catherine stared out to the pool, still bothered by questions. Henri reached to his pocket for his cigarettes, freezing at Catherine's reaction.

'*Et alors?* So I smoke? You hate it, yes? You are a true *poken!*'

'It's so disgusting!' Catherine shot back, surprised by her own candour.

Henri laughed. '*Bien sûr, c'est dégueulasse!* And so bad for your health. I'm sorry to offend you. Here, choose a dessert!' he insisted, tapping the menu. 'You must have a vice too. Something creamy or sweet. All the tourists get fat here in New Caledonia on the *mousse au chocolat!*'

Catherine reddened.

'I know the *chef* of the *tribu*, if you want to meet him,' he suggested, thankfully changing the subject.

'Wouldn't it seem like sticky-beaking?'

'Not really. He – or someone there may know something.'

At that particular moment, full of *terrine* and *entrecôte maison* and contemplating a *crème caramel*, Catherine didn't have the energy to make a decision one way or the other. It was starting to drizzle with rain. He was surely bragging about meeting the *chef*, the leader of the clan. Showing off. She switched her thoughts to how nice it would be to have a dip in the pool, even in the rain, or a siesta in the little hut.

'We must be going,' Henri announced. 'We have lost time now that I entertain you here.'

'Let me pay for this, at least my share,' said Catherine.

But Henri wouldn't hear of it. They returned to the car, Catherine walking slightly ahead, at once touched and unsettled by his generosity.

In the early years Robert would thrill to hunting. Watching them drag the slain animal from the back of the ute, slinging it up over the frame of *gaiac* to let it bleed into the already-red dirt. He hangs around, watching the men return with their manfulness, their sense of affair, their hunter's pride sitting, tempered, on their shoulders. The ritual is ingrained in his bones, and he finds himself longing for his try with the rifle, though he is still a way yet from this rite of passage.

When he is allowed to go, he sits excitedly in the back of the pick-up with his step-brothers. Gaëtan's voice is always rougher, packed with his companions in the front seat, driving through the half-light before dawn, to the scene of the shoot.

Yet at the same time he can't deny what he feels, watching, as mother and fawn look up, nervously, in the way such creatures do when their senses alert them to human presence. A little further away, the stag, less sensitive to sound this time, reliant on the female, but finally, also looking. If only he need not kill the deer. Of their gentleness, especially their eyes, he tells no one; he knows the jeering response it will draw.

If only, instead of a rifle, he could point a camera. He could muffle its whirring under his coat. Instead of a shot and the slow contortion of muscle and limb as life saps heavily to the ground, why not a record of beauty and vigour, a unit of family, mother and father, child. Would he not be admired for this feat, for his skill in capturing this tender moment before death?

But no. Such sentiments are unknown, or if known, unexpressed. And doesn't he too feel the thrill at the chase, the will to capture, if not to beat? Doesn't he too eat the *cerf* at table, and fight for the right to give the bone to the smallest dog? No, his thoughts cannot be shared, not even with Dominique, for the meat is staple, or so he is told when one day, feigning curiosity, he raises the issue.

One season, it is true, they slaughter more cattle than they sell, and it seems they eat pickled meat for months. Only later he finds it is because the animals are going lame – their tendons have been cut. It is 1982: the start of the groundswell against white-owned farms on the north-east coast. Already a few farmers are starting to consider their options: sell back to the state and flee to Nouméa, or pitch in and resist the claims to the land on which they have settled.

'Third generation, *moi*, I die here.' Gaëtan's words.

At first it is easy to be proud like that. But the mood is changing. Unease is creeping into the *caldoche* community with the growth of new political parties and new ideas: land rights, independence. Truths and myths are bandied about and the divide between the landed and the dispossessed grows deeper and wider. Gaëtan's farm borders on the boundaries of three different *tribus*. Two pro-independence, the third neutral, edging to loyalist. As time goes on it will no longer be possible to hide in the shades of grey; the new politics push everyone to manifest a clear alliance with one or other of the positions. You are either for or against independence from France, and everything that goes with it.

1982. The year Robert turns twelve. It has taken twelve years for his identity to form to this point. In the next six years, how can he know that it will start to deform, to blow about hollowly in the unresting winds of his embittered country? How can he know?

———

Approaching Canala the landscape transformed from lush green into a red and scarred terrain, cat-scratched by mining exploitation, the hills terraced into sores of concentric circles and rivulets.

There was little sign of life, hardly a signpost, and even when they finally arrived in the town, with its faint smell of rotten eggs, no welcoming restaurants or inns. From side-on Catherine could just catch Henri's wry smile, as if he were reading, even relishing her dismay.

'What is it? Not much like a tourist postcard?'

'Does anyone live here? It just feels so desolate, so isolated.'

'It is.'

'What, isolated?'

'Canala used to be a hub, in the last century – hard to believe isn't it? The first visitors to New Caledonia landed here, looking for sandalwood. Then it became the centre of mining. But it has seen some transformation since that time.' Henri paused, stroking the top of his lip. 'That is why I'm here,' he continued. 'To help process some of the past, let them give expression to things that happened.'

'What things?'

'Canala was the seat of conflict during *les événements*. It was here that Machoro macheted the ballot box to boycott the territorial elections. The FLNKS – the Kanak independence front – wanted only Kanaks to vote. They were the minority, they didn't feel they had a voice. Do you remember that?'

Catherine confessed her ignorance.

'He was shot, in the end,' said Henri, 'by gendarmes, like I told you. He had held the town of Thio to ransom for three weeks. He was a problem for France.'

She said nothing. She couldn't work out Henri's take on the matter. He seemed sympathetic to both sides, if there *were* two sides. Even that wasn't clear.

'Is the article for *Le Journal*?'

Henri gave her a sidelong glance. 'Now that would be telling.'

She decided to let it drop. 'But what do people *do* here now?'

'They mine. They work, they eat, they sleep. Like you and me,' he added, another oblique smile punctuating the seriousness.

They passed the village, then Henri turned south along a dirt road. The mountains looked bare and gouged, almost decapitated in parts. They climbed up for a few kilometres as the afternoon sun moved down in the sky.

'I guess you know where you're going.'

'Don't worry.' He still had the corners of a smile about his mouth. Catherine tried to feel reassured by his confidence, pushing away misgivings about the wisdom of going bush like this.

'Relax,' Henri said, as if he had noticed. 'We're nearly there.'

As they climbed the last few metres the bay came into view, wide and open. Where the hills had been razed and dotted with sparse, stunted trees, the colours of the landscape were now returning to lush green as they headed deeper into the valley. Turning, Catherine saw the cascade, like a surprise, as if planted for her as an antidote to the desolation.

'You can swim if you like. It's all right, there is nothing to bite!'

How strange to have dreamt exactly this fantasy – to swim in an isolated pool at the top of a waterfall. She could never have imagined it arriving for her in such a form, such an oasis of beauty, so deep and hidden in this remote, harsh valley, and wild, as if she were the first to discover it.

'Are you going in?' she ventured.

'*Vas-y*, you go.'

She was glad he let her swim alone. Just at that moment she could not have withstood the tension of having him so close in the water.

───◌───

The secondary school on the west coast is run by the Brothers who do their best to provide a balance of theory and practical, a program they claim meets the intellectual, practical and spiritual needs of their students. Technical studies form a big part of the curriculum. Obviously, the boys need to know how engines, cars and farm machinery work. But their liberal arts philosophy also allocates time to languages, music, literature and history. Those who finish are considered to be well-rounded on their graduation after the *troisième*.

The school suits Robert, who surprises himself with his interest in French literature. At the same time he is practically minded; handy on the farm and keen to learn more about the physics behind carburettors and crankshafts. Gaëtan has taught him a great deal but now he is learning things he can teach Gaëtan: agriculture and farm economics and animal husbandry. He soaks it up with an energy that pleases his teachers but pitches him unpopularly against his peers.

On weekends Robert has the beautiful beaches of La Roche Percée and Turtle Bay to explore; he can fish, ride his old bike around, or snorkel in the lagoon. Of course, he misses home and he misses Rosina and her family. Frédéric is his only really good friend. He doesn't feel he fits into the groups which seem to form naturally but unfairly according to ethnic background. Robert isn't as big as the Wallis Islanders, neither his hands nor his shoulders can match the span of his Polynesian classmates. Robert feels different from both groups and floats between them.

Most of the students board with relatives; a few, like Robert, with local families, returning home on long weekends and holidays. Not many of the boys continue. After the *troisième* class, most leave school for jobs. Some make it to the seminary in Nouméa, a few to the *lycée*. Even those who want to continue need to have a family in Nouméa who will take them.

'You'll have to think about that,' says Robert's teacher, one time in *quatrième*. He remembers the day; the rains have swollen the river to overflowing and the road to the school has been cut off for most of the school population. Down on the beach at La Roche, people have said, the causeway has even washed away completely, cutting off the peninsula and making it an island. The army has been called in to ferry the stranded residents across to get provisions from the village.

Robert is one of the few to make it to class, and finds himself the only student in *littérature*.

'Eh bien,' announces Monsieur Leblanc. 'Perhaps today we will not be continuing our discussion of *Le Petit Prince*. What would you like to talk about?'

Robert, shy of his teacher's confidence, gives a shrug.

'What about *you* then?' continues Monsieur Leblanc. 'Your plans? You're doing well. Do you plan to go to Nouméa to try for your baccalauréat, or do you have other ideas?'

Robert starts in surprise.

'I – I don't think I'll be going on, Monsieur.'

'Why not? You're one of the top students. Haven't you thought about it? What do your parents say?'

Robert thinks of Gaëtan and Dominique, the two of them, repairing the hen coop, tending the vegetable patch, fixing the fences, feeding cattle, rounding them for castration or slaughter, surviving, merely, and keeping them all alive.

'I suppose I'll go back and work on the farm. Gaëtan is getting on . . .'

'But Robert, there is no future for you there, surely you must know that. It is finished, *les caldoches* on the east coast. Gaëtan is one of the few who hangs on, I don't know if it's stubbornness or faith or stupidity.'

Robert lifts his eyes to his teacher's, meeting the puzzled gaze of another *caldoche*. His frankness is unsettling.

He has of course been aware of the tension, overheard discussions at home of the isolation of the farm, a white farm on a *terre revendiquée* – subject to a land rights' claim – and Gaëtan now the last remaining *caldoche* in the immediate area.

'Politics or no politics, you need to think of your own future,' Monsieur Leblanc continues. 'Who do you know in Nouméa? You must go to the *lycée*, absolutely. In fact, I wonder if you could apply for a scholarship or something?'

'What would I do?' says Robert shyly. Though he enjoys studying, he can see no purpose in the endless pursuit of French literature or *histoire–géo*. He is conscious of his good marks, and values his teachers' comments, gathering them carefully and painstakingly, like scattered jewels into an envelope. But to what end and to what purpose? For Robert, they are an end in themselves. He never for a moment has imagined continuing further than the *troisième*, knowing no one in Nouméa with whom he could board.

'Do? Well, of course, you should decide on a stream. But you could go on to university, you know there is the new one opening its doors in Nouméa the year after next. Just in time for you.'

'University?' Now Robert is really struggling. What does one do at university?

'You could do law, or arts or languages – you're not bad at English,' Monsieur Leblanc continues. 'Or else you could apply to go to France if, say, you wanted to do engineering or architecture or something like that.'

Robert's head is reeling. He has imagined such a small future, such a local world, the world at his doorstep, the only world he knows, and to which he has clung so tenaciously. He can't help thinking of Rosina. Where in all this would she fit? Does she plan to go to Nouméa to finish her studies, envisage university? Robert doubts it. The pull of her family is too strong.

'Would you like me to find out about scholarships at least? It would cover your costs in Nouméa, say, if you boarded with a family. What do you think?'

'Sure, yes, sure,' says Robert, more to end the conversation than as a gesture of commitment. He can no more imagine leaving Gaëtan or Rosina than being elected *Président de la République*. But if it pleases his teacher he'll apply for the scholarship.

'That's organised then,' says Monsieur Leblanc. 'I'll let you know. There'll be papers for your parents to sign.'

———

Henri watched Catherine wade into the rock pool. He didn't feel like swimming. In truth he was troubled by his passage into this terrain, a part of the country he had not visited since those tumultuous days a decade ago.

1984. December, when the *flamboyants* bloom, bleed their red flowers over the land. The Hienghène massacre. 1985, January. The season of the fires, white settlers' properties burnt, their owners fleeing the bush for the *caldoche* stronghold of Nouméa. The boy, the young *lycéen*, home for the holidays, working on the family property, killed by a single shot to the head by a sniper. His death unleashing anger and pandemonium in small-town Nouméa and throughout the country. Unlike any conflict Henri had witnessed, not even in Algiers, or Paris. He can still see the shocked, white-angry faces of the young *lycéens* from Boulouparis and La Foa, joining their fellow students in the streets, at the gates of the High Commission, trying to pass under the metal bars with cries of *'Pisani assassin!'*

Pisani, Mitterand's personal delegate, heralded as an exceptional negotiator. Not to the palate of the *caldoches*, since he had tried to negotiate with the Kanak independence front, the FLNKS.

So pro-independence houses had burnt in the night, the pharmacy, also *indépendantiste*, smashed, everything thrown from its window. Every visible stone, down to the marble from the Bank of Indochina, seized, pelted at the CRS – the special forces, reinforcements who had arrived with the paratroopers and forty more journalists from France, since a state of emergency had been declared. The two days of rioting and chaos, checked momentarily, tensely, by the 'neutralisation' of the radical FLNKS leader and his deputy just two days later.

He, Henri Boulez, *correspondant politique*, had chronicled it all.

Had it stopped there? Not for another four years, at least, and then more. Not even now, not yet.

No, Henri didn't feel like swimming here.

They had come to a small, rundown dwelling with rusted corrugated iron sheets falling from its roof. 'Jim' – a wiry septuagenarian in a singlet and baggy shorts with braces – opened the door, such as it was, and waved them inside.

At first Catherine wondered whether Jim would talk at all for Henri's article. He mumbled an offer of coffee and concentrated on its preparation; hand-grinding the beans, shuffling slowly between sink and oven-top, whistling while it brewed. His face was sun-weathered, not unfriendly but, she guessed, probably not used to smiling.

She took her lead from Henri, whose silence seemed to respect the significance of the ceremony. She sat on the single creaking chair at the tin-topped table and waited for Jim to start the conversation. Henri was still standing.

'Up from Nouméa this morning?' Jim said finally. His front teeth were missing and his words were slurred. He poured the thick coffee into enamel mugs and pushed a bowl of sugar and a tin of powdered milk towards them.

'How long has your family been here, Jim, in the region?' asked Henri.

Jim didn't answer, fossicking about under the table for something to sit on.

'Here,' he said to Henri, pulling out a wobbly stool.

'Please, no, you take that,' said Henri. 'I can stand.'

Jim settled himself. 'Now, what was that you said?'

'Tell us about your life, how you came to be here.'

Jim looked at Henri directly for the first time.

'My grandfather came in 1895 from Alsace,' he said slowly. 'He was given the land, further north. By Gouverneur Feillet. It was too close to the river. At the first cyclone he had to move higher up on the banks. Two, three cyclones, each time higher.' Jim illustrated his story with jerky arm gestures. 'By the fourth he left to find work in the mines, at Thio.'

'My father returned to the land. He wanted to be a stockman.' Jim paused, staring through the dirty windowpane. 'She's a *poken*, you say?' he said, jabbing a finger at Catherine. 'She'll know what I mean. Brought down a thousand head of cattle from the north. Set himself up. Built the fences and corrals himself, with the station hands. The Kanaks are good with horses.' The spittle was gathering at the corners of his mouth. 'You had to do it all with strong wood – there were wild bulls around.'

'When were you born?'

'In 1920. It was *"la crise"*. My father became a butcher – all the locals told him they needed him!' Jim's face crinkled with laughter. 'But he couldn't sell in the open-air markets. So he took a bike with a basket in front and went from property to property. "Roger Léon – *bonne viande, beau bétail!*"' Jim nearly fell off the stool as he demonstrated. 'We still had our land, back then, before *les événements*. I was one of a big family, we all worked on it.'

'And – on your mother's side?' Henri said carefully.

'My mother married the son of a *communard*.'

'Political prisoners from Paris,' Henri explained to Catherine. 'Sent to the penal colonies on the islands, some here on the mainland.'

Jim continued his pioneering stories, speaking with emphasis but without sentimentality. Henri prompted thoughtfully, allowing the old man time to reflect. He took no notes. Catherine wasn't sure if he had got to the main point of his visit.

She watched as Jim rose, a little shaky on his feet, suggesting a *sirop de menthe*. Henri began pacing, his hand gestures becoming more expansive. They must have started talking about *les événements*.

'Land! *La terre!*' Jim was spluttering. 'I'll tell you about land. Where the Kanaks had their terraces of taro and yam, yes, our grandfathers tried to plant corn and vegetables, lucerne and rice. But they had the heat, the cyclones, the locusts, that meant it was never profitable. They battled with the floods, the vines, the mosquitoes and thistles, the wasps.' His eyes grew watery. 'And *we* lived off nothing. Three kilos of onions, a litre of oil and two kilos of coffee, my wife used to say, we raised three children on that.'

It seemed Henri had hit the target; no more polite questions.

'How can you say we stole the land?' Jim continued, steadying himself with one hand on the stool, unwilling to sit back down.

'I'm not saying you stole it,' Henri replied. 'I'm voicing the arguments of your critics – the circumstances of history, of colonisation. For the Kanaks, land is organic, sacred; man is integrated with it, belongs to it, not the other way around. It is still something very different, you must agree, for the *caldoches*. Is it any wonder there was such mistrust when the Kanaks saw their land used for profit, packaged, numbered off, sold? What do you say to that?'

'Pah!' Jim banged his glass of *menthe* on the table and pointed a finger at Henri. 'What you z'*oreilles* don't understand back in your offices is that we who *live* on the land – *we* know it, we understand it. We breathe it, shovel it, care for it. It sticks to our fingers, we know its colour, its form, its smell. I'm not packing my bags. I've lived through the siege of Thio, the fall of Machoro. *Je suis chez moi.*'

Catherine was starting to feel sleepy – she must have eaten too much lunch. She was trying to follow the rapid French, to recall the historical events, but the names and places were from a foreign world.

Henri seemed to be trying to summarise Jim's position. 'So what you're saying, Jim, is that, above all, we must not buckle to the *marchands*, nor to the demagogues . . .'

'I haven't changed towards the Kanaks. They leave me my peace – I leave them theirs.'

And as suddenly as it had stirred, the passion of the argument diminished. Jim showed no ill-will, looked more as if he had gained a new respect for Henri. It was what she liked so much about the French; something she knew had been suppressed in her conversion to the Australian way of arguing. If you disagreed with another's politics you kept your distance. Here, it enriched your relationship.

'Do you like horses?' Henri was asking.

And Jim was off again, slapping his stomach as he recalled the names of the horses. 'Fleur de lune! A phenomenon! Tabarong, always the last to go and the first to cross the finishing line. Figaro. Bagatelle. A stud!'

'Horse-racing? Are you talking about horse racing?' asked Catherine. They were the first words she had spoken in two hours. 'Did you – I wonder if you would have known a Georges Ransan? He worked at Poro on the mines?'

'Ransan,' said Jim, screwing up his eyes. 'Yeah, I knew a Ransan – Georges, you say? A regular at the races. *Les courses de brousse* at Houilou, La Foa, Bourail.'

Catherine stared in disbelief. 'Yes, that's him,' she said, incredulous. 'You knew him?'

'Oh, *comme-ci comme-ça*, you know, not well, kept to ourselves you know. Think he came down from Tiébaghi when it shut. Don't know what became of him. Might still be there, who knows?'

Henri shrugged, giving Catherine a crooked smile. 'I told you it wouldn't be hard to find out something!'

'How far is it to Poro?' said Catherine. 'Could we continue on?'

'Well . . . I should be getting back.'

Once more, Catherine felt her vulnerability to the whims of chance. She didn't want to plead, and yet the discovery left her even more determined.

'Isn't there any public transport, a bus or something?'

Jim snorted. 'Out here? 'You must be joking!'

'*Allez*, it's possible,' Henri said. '*On continue*. Let's go.'

They found a half-decent meal of *steak-frites* at the next village, sharing the bar with an assortment of miners, the variety of faces, under the red dirt, a mirror to the mixture of ethnicities in the mining industry.

Catherine was tired. She wanted to be alone, to read, to think. Henri wanted to make some notes for his article and bid her goodnight.

Later, after showering and on her way back to her room, Catherine stopped. It was so still; only the occasional chirrup of cicadas or the whine of mosquitoes. A little away, standing with his back to her was Henri, the shadow of his body leaning against the wall of his box-like room. She thought of his argument today with Jim. His zeal, his expressiveness. He'd been convincing. As she watched, plumes of smoke seemed to rise from him. In the moonlight it looked as if he might be burning silently. Like some kind of totem, a mysterious statue in the dark. She waited a moment longer, wondering who would move first. Henri finished his cigarette, tossed it in a predictable gesture into the surrounding bush and faded into his room.

They have always danced together, especially at family celebrations, but now when Rosina dances he feels her smile is only for him. He feels he could watch her forever, so magnificent is she when she dances, her hips circling hypnotically and her strong legs stamping, her upper body so controlled, so expertly still.

But he feels self-conscious, staring at her; better to join her on the floor, show her how to dance the rock, the routine he has learnt from her brothers and which, by a stroke of luck, he has mastered. It suits his style, the quick energy and the tight steps. Rosina in turn gives the impression – whether she is indulging him or not – of being impressed at his dancing. He can't wait to fling her out and pull her back to him, to have his body touch hers if he pulls her closer than usual, to know it is only a millimetre of cloth that separates their skin. He wants to feel her laughter in his face and to hold her smile, the smile he has designated as his. To him she is light and solid at the same time; light as a swallow dipping away and back, and yet full and strong and solid as the earth.

Twelve

'Like being in boarding school again,' Catherine said the next morning.

Henri looked up from his bowl of café au lait. 'What was?'

'Having the washrooms miles from where you sleep.'

'You were in boarding school too?'

'Not the happiest experience of my life, but yes.'

'How old?'

'From eight. After the fire my mother couldn't keep me . . .'

Somehow, thousands of kilometres away and her mother in her grave, it was as if she had permission to be bitter.

'And your sister?'

'She stayed with my mother. My mother considered her a fragile child. She used to do things like hold her breath till she was blue in the face when she couldn't have what she wanted. Then, literally, she would pass out. My mother would go into hysterics. She'd call an ambulance, and every time Vivi would just pull out of it.'

'Sounds very manipulative.'

'It was exactly that. My sister was exactly that.'

'And now?'

'And now . . .' Catherine stopped, the memory of the Paris trip too fresh. 'She hasn't changed, I don't think.'

'How long were you in boarding school?'

'At fifteen I won a scholarship to England. I never returned to France after that, not to live.'

'So then you became English.'

'I suppose, yes.'

'*Allons*,' Henri said abruptly, but she was expecting it.

'*En route*,' she finished.

They are usually alone at Turtle Beach. The descent down the craggy track is too steep for vehicles. Most of the locals prefer the whiter, more open beach at La Roche Percée. And it is early, dawn. Too early for most of the usuals.

Frédéric has a board he's found in a shed in the village. He can't believe his luck. They don't recognise the brand name but it isn't French. They think it must have belonged to Rouquin, the mechanic, who used to go back and forth to Australia. Rouquin used to brag about the '*Gol Cos*', a place called Surfer's Paradise. To the boys it sounds like a far-flung diamond paradise, a frontier of unimaginable pleasure and sophistication. They do not know it is only two hours away in a plane. They associate that part of the world with the muttered history of blackbirding, the *kanakas* from their islands who were shipped over to labour in the sugar cane fields.

Robert has fashioned a home-made board from a plank of driftwood, smoothed into a V-shape, perfect for sliding along under the curl of the surf.

It's choppy, the water looks darker as the sun rises behind them, the colour beyond the reef a deeper indigo than the usual turquoise. They wait in the shallows a while, Robert bracing against the whip of salt on his skin, Frédéric because he's still not used to the sport.

'*Allez* – chicken!' Frédéric teases Robert. 'Go!'

Robert pushes under with his board. A second later he surfaces just under the curl of the wave. He springs upright and balances expertly on the board, a streak of smooth mahogany. He holds it a second, then the board flips up and his arms flail as he's dumped.

'Robert!' calls Frédéric, laughing. He watches, expecting him to surface in the next second. The wave heaves back, and suddenly it's loud around him, the wind claps his ears.

'Robert!' Frédéric can't see him, and starts wading towards where he saw him go down. He tosses his board behind him as he tries to stride forward in the thick water.

'Robert,' he calls again. 'Mate, where are you?'

Just as he calls he collides with something. Panicking now, he feels in the swirl. It is his friend, heavy under water.

With a force spurred by adrenalin Frédéric manages to lift the weight. One look at Robert's face and he knows he's been knocked out. Frédéric shakes him, the fear taking hold, then another wave knocks them both forward. It all happens so quickly. Frédéric manages to get back up, keeping hold of his friend. He must have been out for only a few seconds, enough to drown and yet he's not dead – *he can't be dead* – and the mixed flood of not knowing and panic almost sickens him.

They are not so far out and Frédéric makes it to the beach. He knows what to do, he may not have done much surfing but he's grown up around boats and fishing and men falling overboard with too much alcohol. After the water is disgorged and a few breaths pumped into his chest, Robert comes to. His body stiffens in the recovery position, and he splutters.

'So much for your marvellous board, *mon vieux*,' says Frédéric, the trembling humour a thin disguise for shock. 'Given you a nice knockout, hey!'

Robert can't speak. He is disoriented, dazed.

'How the hell am I going to get you back up?' says Frédéric.

They sit, slumped together in silence. Frédéric starts to shiver, though it is not cold. It seems the danger has passed. Frédéric knows he should get Robert to the clinic, but he also knows they'll be in trouble. They shouldn't have been doing this in the first place.

He is still working on a plan to get Robert back when he hears them.

Soft crunching sounds on the sand and a swish as they move up the beach. The creatures move past the human statues, oblivious to them, like a gesture of trust.

Huge, silent turtles, climbing far up the beach to lay their eggs.

By the time Dr Bernard sees them at the clinic, Robert seems quite back to normal, just a little sleepy. The doctor looks into his pupils, checks his ears, slaps him on the back and tells him he's a fool.

'You were lucky, young man. What were you doing down there? You must be mad to throw yourselves into that surf. Too many rips, far too dangerous. Anyway, isn't it a school day? You two should be in class. Off you go, stop taking up my time.'

They have left their bikes down at the beach, having hitched a lift back to the village. So now it is off to the college, another two kilometres out of the village, on foot.

They flag down another lift, this time the local transporter, who hauls his huge truck to a halt.

'You boys in trouble or something?' he says, but laughs. 'Or off to the military base for some tougher discipline?'

They try to sneak into class after the morning break. But one of the Brothers notices and they are in detention after school.

Robert hasn't been able to concentrate all day. The emotion rests hard as a stone in his chest. *I am alive*, he thinks. *I nearly died.* These are my hands, they are the same hands, the same colour, not changed. My arms, they move, I can breathe. *What must it be like to be dead?* Cold, it must be cold, whatever else it is. And I am not cold, I am warm and alive and sitting here, writing lines while the teacher busies himself with preparation, oblivious to the fact that I'm *not dead.* What will Rosina think when I tell her? She'll be shocked. She will tell me off, tell me I'm crazy. He smiles to himself, thinking of her reaction. It's true, she will care. She will be cross at him, because she cares. He lingers on this thought a little, appreciating the warmth it infuses through his body. It is as if it has never occurred to him. *But I wanted to do it,* he hears himself explaining to her. I wanted to show Frédéric. I want to be the first to surf here, I want to show everyone. No one else knows anything about surfing, about the massive magic waves in Australia they will see, together, one day.

'Naudin, get on with your lines.'

Robert realises he has been staring at the Brother. He drops his head quickly, makes writing gestures over his paper.

'I was just thinking, Monsieur.'

'Well, think about writing, will you, or we'll be here all night.'

Robert finishes the sentence and looks over at Frédéric. He is copying lines, boredom and fatigue seep from every cell in his body. Frédéric. *He saved my life. If he hadn't been there I would be dead.* Robert's hand is frozen in mid-air as he takes in the face of his friend, a face so strangely unmoved. He seems to have forgotten he is a hero, has shrugged off any fuss. *He saved my life, and there he is, writing lines.*

'Robert, you'll be doing another two pages if you don't keep writing. Move it, lad.'

Robert is stuck in a conflict of desire to say something to Frédéric. He knows it would be stupid, embarrassing, and more than that, it would earn them both another detention. He realises he has no words anyway for such an event. What do you say to someone who saves your life? Words and feelings lurch in his chest with clumsy, vague definition. It is like a kind of love, the feeling you have about someone who saves your life. Surely, that is it. But at the same time he sweats with embarrassment at the thought. What words could express such gratitude? Of course, there are none. To say anything would seem trivial.

Overcome suddenly, his eyes well up with tears. He can't stop them now, they splash onto his paper, smudging the lines. He is thirteen and crying, in front of the other boys. The teacher moves to reprimand him again. But the words stop in his throat as Robert stands abruptly, knocking his chair over.

'You don't understand. No one understands. You don't know what it's like to be *here*, alive.' His voice is thick with emotion, but the teacher has no idea what he is talking about.

Robert turns to run out of the classroom. No one moves to stop him, they can only watch, nonplussed.

'Frédéric, thank you,' he shouts from outside the door. 'It will never be enough, but thank you.'

And he runs, out of the school, out onto the road, back to the village, back along the road to the now darkening beach, where he wants to sit for a long time gazing at the white curl of surf as the sun sets. He sits and thinks about life, about death, about love and the stars and the sky and about the acid-edged joy of being alive.

Thirteen

It was well after noon when they chanced upon the nurse from the clinic in the town of Poro. They had tried the post office, where the young clerk had looked up at them sleepily, lifted his eyebrows and shrugged his shoulders. The freshly showered, crisp-shirted young officer at the gendarmerie had spun them the official line. He was not, *désolé*, Monsieur and Madame, able to release any personal details of anyone passing through. If they wanted to file a missing persons claim they could fill in this form. Henri had glanced at his watch. Impatient, or hungry, it meant the same thing. It was time to leave.

The nurse, a woman in her forties, was finishing her shift. On first impression, clacking efficiently along the passage, she looked as though she was not about to let enquiring foreigners delay her. Catherine excused herself for the bad timing before announcing the purpose of their visit.

Perhaps it was the name, or something about the way Catherine pronounced it, that caused the nurse to pause.

'I remember a Ransan. Yes, of course I knew him. Bit of a loner. No family. A few years back now. Came in one time badly beaten up. We had to send him on to Bourail, to assess if he needed to go down to Nouméa.'

Catherine felt Henri's hand on her shoulder, a light touch.

'Do you know what happened after?' she asked.

'Think they treated him in Bourail. Something about his eye. There were others as well from the *tribu*. Seems they got into a fight. Something about a girl from the *tribu*. Don't know much more than that.'

'Did he return here? Do you know anything more?'

The nurse frowned. 'I don't remember seeing him again, but that doesn't mean he didn't come back. No, I don't remember, I'm sorry. I remember that he used to come and go a bit. Think he was back and forth to Australia even.'

Catherine nodded.

'You might find out more in Bourail. You know, over there on the west coast. My sister works at the clinic there.'

Henri nodded, drawing the conversation to a close.

'I've got contacts in Bourail,' he said as he steered Catherine to the door. 'Let's go back and you can plan the next stage of your search.'

'Thank you,' said Catherine to the nurse. 'Please, what is your name? We didn't ask.'

'Nicole,' she said. 'Nice to have met you.'

—⁙—

It is dusk when they reach the half-way mark along the Col des Roussettes, the road that crosses the mountains to the east coast. Robert has tried not to show his impatience; there is equipment to pack away at school, preparations for Monday. He helps of course, he never needs to be asked.

It is generous of Monsieur Leblanc to offer him a lift. Otherwise he has to take the long, sluggish trip by bus, up and down the steep gradients of the Col. Lately, no one is sure whether the bus is running at all.

It is a privilege of sorts to travel back with Monsieur Leblanc. He's a local, his family owns a garage in Houailou, on the east coast, on the other side of the pass. Robert is allowed to call him Michel, it being the weekend.

Gaëtan will be there for him on the other side, he is never late. He'll take him on up the coast in the darkness to the farm. Tomorrow there'll be fishing, maybe this weekend the calf will finally arrive, and tomorrow too, he'll see Rosina.

There are hardly any cars on the road. The tourists have stopped coming completely, warned that it is not safe. Michel keeps his eyes intently ahead while Robert checks out to the sides. Usually they travel in silence; tonight is no exception. They have said all they need to about Robert's schoolwork, his plans for next year. Now there is the next stretch of the pass to get through, past some of the tribal land.

The first stone hits after the river bend, just as they come through a clump of bamboos. It booms; at first Robert thinks a tyre has blown. The next one hits the windscreen, making a small, webbing crack. Robert raises his arms to shield his face, then moves to protect his teacher. But Michel is hitting the brakes, abruptly enough to send the car into a skid. Another hail of smaller stones, thankfully hitting the sides.

'Keep down!' calls Robert.

'No,' says Michel. 'Not this time. Not again.'

The tyres grind into the dirt as he pulls up and yanks the handbrake. The car has jack-knifed and rests across the road. Anyone coming from either direction could crash into it. Michel strides off. Robert is too stunned for a moment to move.

There is a scatter of brown legs, a sandal drops into the dust and then – *laughter?*

'Stay there,' Michel calls back.

'Where are you going?'

'To see the *chef*, you stay there.'

'Wait, I'll come too.'

'Safer in the car.'

Robert catches up with Michel standing a little away from the entrance to the *grande case*. As far as he can tell, Michel has already found the *chef* and is deep in discussion with him. It is hard to pick the mood. It feels uneasy. Michel is throwing his arms about, his voice is raised, his words carry outrage. This is politics, Robert knows. But something more, as well.

Then he realises. The two men know each other. Michel used to teach in these parts, before he took the position in Bourail. They share a past, and the roots of a friendship planted long before these times of division and violence.

'Whose kid was it?' he can hear Michel saying. 'Do they not have the courage to face me now?'

Robert hangs back; it is not his fight. Fear gives way to the outrage of injustice. Michel's windscreen will have to be replaced. They will be late. Gaëtan will be worried. All this, for politics.

He can see the *chef* trying to calm Michel. His hand rests on Michel's shoulder. He looks as if he is trying to gather him up, to walk forward together. Yes, he will find the kids who did it. Yes, they were both born here. Yes, there should be another way.

Abruptly Michel turns around and points back at Robert. 'And him, what about him?' His voice is still indignant. 'You know what I stand for. But what about him? He was born here too. Where do you live when you are both black and white? Whose side are you on?'

Robert reddens, feels naked, exposed.

'It is not about black and white,' the *chef* is saying. 'It is not that, you have not understood.'

'Independence, land, colonisation, emancipation . . .' the words drop into centre stage, the flags of unending struggle.

'Does that give your children the right to stone my car?' Michel continues. 'I taught them to read. *I* did. Don't tell me they made a mistake with the car. It doesn't matter *who* was in the car.'

Robert shifts from foot to foot. Where *does* he stand? They are both of them right.

Children start to appear, three or four of them, pushing each other forward. From other dwellings he sees men and women coming out, young men with headbands in red, yellow, black and green. They observe the scene, uneasy. Threat is building. Someone, anyone, could have a gun. Robert wants to leave, to reach the coast, to see Gaëtan. He feels a child still, despite his fourteen years. The complexities, the problem, the solution of independence – all escape his grasp. And, childishly, he can view it only from his perspective. Having found a home, all he wants is to stay in it. But having found a home, he is being told that it was never his to have.

Some of the young men are circling around Michel. This Robert recognises, this he understands, and more quickly than Michel. The prelude to violence, Robert knows it; it is stored in his body, like a memory under skin.

'Monsieur Leblanc,' he calls, his voice sounding thin. 'Leave it. Let's go, it's getting dark.'

Violence – an expression, a response, not an answer. This Dominique has taught him. There are other ways, other answers. Now is not the time, not now, not here.

Michel turns to Robert, taking in his expression: part-fear, part-defiance. Part naked, naïve courage.

'*Allons*, let's go.'

Fourteen

He had touched her shoulder. Only a light touch, but his timing had moved her. It was the moment the nurse had mentioned Georges.

The drive back to Nouméa had been in silence. That was nothing unusual, she was getting used to his style. She thought back to that first lunch together, all that posing and bluff, the candour, the teasing. He had been showing off, surely. Now she felt that she had his measure. The abruptness, the impatience; they concealed a generosity of spirit. Why else would he have prolonged his trip?

She couldn't help being curious about his private life. Was he lonely? *Martine* – the receptionist in his office. Was she his type? Some men were hard to read; hadn't she always got it wrong? Henri had let nothing – hardly anything – slip. She'd found out he must have been married before, at least that he had a child – grown-up, living in France. But he had hardly lingered on those topics. He seemed, now she thought about it, to have always redirected the conversation back to Catherine's life. Was he really interested in her story? Or her? Perhaps it was his curiosity that was so flattering. No one in her circle of friends had ever shown much interest in her life history, though to be fair she was not one to talk freely. Unlike some of her friends back home, she didn't consider unhappy childhoods or failed relationships to be rich conversation topics. For some reason it had been easy to open up to Henri, perhaps because she was a foreigner here and needed him as a contact. But also, she reflected, because he listened without passing judgment or making her feel sorry for herself. He let her talk and he listened.

The sea, behind mountains for most of their return journey, now re-appeared in the distance.

'*Les Alizés?*' said Henri, stirring her from her thoughts.

'Oh . . . yes, that's it.' Catherine hadn't envisaged the end of the journey, the end of their time together.

'I have some things to sort out now. Shall I give you a call?'

'Yes . . . of course.'

The image of the bare hotel room with its empty cupboards took over. Henri seemed business-like and focused on his next task. The séjour was over.

He parked in front of the hotel and, leaving the car running, carried in her bag.

'*Allez*, bye-bye,' he said. Two pecks on the cheeks. The normal, perfunctory *bise*.

'*Allez*,' she echoed brightly. 'Thank you so much, Henri.' It sounded trite.

He was already in his car, checking the rear-vision mirror and changing gears. A brief wave as he drove off.

Catherine turned and made her way to reception. When she looked up it was into Emmanuel's mock-serious face.

'Welcome back, Madame. A good trip?'

'*Très bien,*' she answered, and then, changing to English, 'My key please. Good afternoon.'

They are driving down the coast on the red dirt road. Gaëtan and Dominique sit in the front of the pick-up, Robert is stretched out in the back. The roads are bony with ridges and the tyres hit potholes every twenty metres. Gaëtan swears under his breath, Dominique pats a chastising hand on his thigh.

She glances at Robert in the rear-vision mirror, his long body lolling around with the bucking of the vehicle. She is apprehensive about the forthcoming meeting. From her years of experience she knows, in theory, it should be all right. They have understandings, there is mutual respect and goodwill, all based on years, generations, of living together. Different cultures, side by side in the same country. This will be a reconciliation, a putting to right. You cannot rewrite history. What happened, happened. The first three years of Robert's life were, she reasons, a blank. She remembers the moment now, when he came to them, pushed forward by the social worker who had made the trek up from Nouméa to hand over Robert. She had expected him to withdraw, to cower as she had seen others do, others similarly neglected or abused. But Robert had stood confidently, observing, taking them in, just three years old, appraising them as an older, more secure, well-adjusted child might before deciding whether to take the risk of greeting strangers. They stood back, she and Gaëtan, giving him time. 'Come and look at the new calf,' Gaëtan had said, and offered his hand. At those words the little boy had run into his arms like a lost grandchild returning from a long separation. Dominique had scuffed his hair and he had smiled up at her and at that moment she knew he had not suffered too much damage, whatever his life before had been.

Dominique looks at Robert again to see if she can entice the same smile. Robert looks around, catching her eye in the mirror.

He grins, much as a younger child might at a friend or a peer, not at his own mother.

'How much further?' he mouths.

Dominique stretches her hands to represent a metre, her face signalling 'a lot'. Robert turns away, allowing his legs to flop again with the roll of the ute.

But now a seriousness has come over his face. The fleeting bright smile he has just shared with her, the only mother he has known, perhaps masking a fear of betrayal.

Dominique smiles back to show him it is fine with her. It is all right to be curious, to want to know about your birth family. It is not a betrayal. Their relationship is too strong for that. But inside brews a concoction of anxiety and doubt. *Will he want to return to her?* And, though she is not keen to admit it, there is also a seed of guilt. Should they have done more to find out earlier, to talk about it even when Robert remained silent, once again, through loyalty to them?

She looks across at Gaëtan, at his set mouth. He rarely smiles, even when he is happy. She only knows he is happy if she sees a tiny creasing web at the corner of his eyes. When he is moved, she has seen a single, silent tear pool secretly, before sliding invisibly down a furrow next to his nose. When he is angry, even, he holds back, rarely has she seen him explode. Just a folding of the arms, a blanching of the lips as they thin into the downturn of his mouth, or the rise and fall of his chest which accelerates by a barely perceptible rate. By these small nuances she usually knows exactly the emotion he feels. But now, today, she is not sure.

Gaëtan almost misses the turn-off and swerves around too quickly. He brakes just in time, almost churning up the road-block of branches, tyres and steel debris before them.

'*L'enfoiré!*' Gaëtan swears.

Dominique peers through the windscreen at the roughly painted signs hitched onto the barrage.

Nos terres sans conditions. Our land – without conditions.

There is a single guard, a young Melanesian of twenty or so, balanced on the barrage as if in a hammock. Sweat bathes his bare torso; it is midday. He wears a white headscarf and swings a long-bladed knife, his *sabre d'abatis*, casually, like a billiard cue.

His arms folded at the steering wheel, Gaëtan sends a glance at Dominique that signals rising anger. They knew to expect this. He has told her so, and they have argued about it. The FLNKS are demanding that the referendum on independence be brought forward and that Kanaks only should have the right to vote. The roads are blocked everywhere.

Dominique leans over to address the man through Gaëtan's window. 'We've been invited. Robert in the back is originally from here, though he hasn't visited in a while.'

The man surveys them through the screen. He sees a white middle-aged couple and a young Kanak boy in the back, or he could be *métis*, his hair is wavy and light brown. He looks over the boy, appraising his youth, his demeanour. Then with the merest inclination of his eyebrows he indicates the path on the other side of the barrage. Clearly, they will not be getting through with the pick-up today.

'How far is it to walk?' continues Dominique.

The man shrugs.

'Let's go then,' she says, opening her door. Robert has already jumped down from the back. Only Gaëtan remains at the wheel, his arms folded, his eyes looking ahead to nowhere, his face set as stone.

'Papy, it's okay,' says Robert. 'We are *chez moi*, remember.'

Gaëtan says nothing, his expression a wall of resistance.

'I'm coming,' says Dominique. Gaëtan can wait. 'What choice is there?' she growls, as Gaëtan still does not respond.

Robert hesitates a second, looking back at his father, but Dominique is firm, indicating with a toss of her head that he should come. We have come this far, and not only today, her face says.

'Don't look back,' she says. 'We are expected.'

They pick their way over the barrage and onto the road on the other side. Dominique sets her sights forward, striding a few paces ahead. Robert turns to call back to Gaëtan.

'We won't stay long, Papy. We won't be long.'

Robert is surprised, even shocked by the state of some of the houses. Here and there curling corrugated iron is held down with heavy stones to prevent a roof from peeling off. In places there are only gaping holes. Robert is not used to luxury, far from it. At least we have water and electricity, he tells Dominique.

Robert has brought chocolate and some metres of fabric to give; Dominique has money and packets of cigarettes.

Dominique has the sense that no one has remembered the reason for their visit. Then, seeing the women come forward to look at Robert, she realises she has mistaken indifference for timidity. Here, pain is not seen, not voiced, discernible only in the lowered eyes of the women, or the silence of the elders. In the young men it is boxed-in anger, the smouldering embers of the dispossessed.

They introduce themselves to the group of women.

'This is Robert. He is from this *tribu*, or so we think, originally.'

The women seem neither suspicious nor surprised. One woman indicates with a thrust of her chin the direction of the *grande case* – the *chef*'s dwelling.

'Where, down there?' asks Dominique. No one else has spoken.

They pick their way over a stony, overgrown path. At the entrance to the *case*, thatched and meagrely decorated at the opening below its central *flèche faîtière*, a man sits cross-legged on a mat of woven reeds, daydreaming, or just awoken from a siesta. He re-positions his body as they approach, leaning forward on one upright knee, and regards them with weathered, oily eyes. His skin is stretched, dried and tanned, mapped with a hundred rivulets of sweat.

Dominique pushes Robert forward with the barest nudge of her elbow, then stands apart, bearing the moment for him in her own trembling chest. She has the overwhelming sense that he is truly stolen. How can she take him back, after this?

Robert moves forward and offers his gifts. Dominique holds her breath. She thinks, too late, that she should have schooled him for this moment, but is relieved to watch him act as if by instinct. He has dropped his eyes deferentially, but so too has the *chef*. It is their way, she thinks, and she could not have prepared him better.

'My mother was Clémentine,' she overhears Robert. 'We think. We are not sure.' Dominique sees him tossing his head back to include herself as the 'we'. '*My mother*', he has said. His birth mother, that is the 'mother' he is referring to. There it is, he has said it. I am his adoptive mother, his second, only ever his second mother. Her heart tightens with an emotion of sadness; of course she will grieve the loss this moment brings. To cover the tears seeding in her eyes she steps forward with her offerings, thrusts them into the *chef*'s hands, knows it is clumsy, that she has disturbed the moment.

At the mention of Clémentine, the old man lifts his chin and tells him to go back to the women.

Somehow, the women have understood. Dominique wonders how they have managed to communicate so soundlessly and so rapidly. She is not even sure what passed between Robert and the *chef*, but she sees him suddenly pulled into the women's circle as one by one they embrace him, unable to drop his hand once it is grasped. One by one, they look quickly into his face, smile, then look away.

A man stands nearby, watching the women, unable to come close. Perhaps it is Robert's uncle, thinks Dominique, with the special status that confers. His role of mentor and guide, also, stolen from him by the circumstances of Robert's birth. She is overwhelmed suddenly by the enormity of their differences; the gulf between their means of communication, the secret, wordless language of the *tribu* which keeps her apart, prevents her from entering their world to discover what she would understand to be satisfying as the 'truth' – the facts of the story which come clapping now at her ears. *Was* Clémentine his mother? Does anyone know? How would they know? How would they prove it? What happened with Robert's father? Was he really beaten up and if so, by whom? Was the girl driven from them?

And then, she thinks, in the end the answers to these questions do not matter. Not in the same way that they matter for her. Theirs is not the same hierarchy of father, mother, brother, sister. For them, connection is enough. They *are*, all of them, Robert's family. He is as much a child of the *tribu* as he identifies himself to be, and as much as they are willing to accept him. This is enough for them, and for him. Perhaps it should be enough for her as well.

It is past one o'clock when they return to Gaëtan. He is leaning against the ute, clearly agitated. As they return he grabs Dominique, a little too hastily, almost roughly, and pushes her inside. Robert is surprised.

'You too, in front.'

The young Kanak on the barrage surveys them departing. He

does not appear to have changed his position. But the humiliation of sitting under his hot eyes for an hour is surely the reason for Gaëtan's vitriol as they speed off.

It is breakfast on Saturday of the long weekend. The boys are up later than usual. Dominique has already left to shop in the village. Gaëtan sits at the table dipping bread into his bowl of coffee. Jean-Paul and Didier hunch wordlessly beside him. The only sounds are chewing, the occasional slurp.

Standing just beside Gaëtan, Robert yawns and stretches like a cat. Gaëtan looks up surprised. He is standing closer than usual.

Gaëtan clears his throat. He looks at the changeling boy, half-man, half-child still, a shadow of fine dark hair fluffed on his top lip.

'Can we go fishing today?' says Robert.

Gaëtan turns back to his coffee. 'I've got to help Maurice.'

'Oh, the elections.'

'Tomorrow maybe.'

'I wanted to go today, now.'

'Thought you'd gone off it. You didn't want to go last time.'

'I had this . . . dream.'

'A dream.'

The statement provokes a loud laugh from Jean-Paul. 'Omens!'

'What do you mean omens?' says Robert, his face still serious.

'People don't talk about dreams, Bobo, it's dumb.'

'So what if it's dumb?'

'What did you dream?' interrupts Gaëtan.

'Nothing.'

'I don't see what dreams have got to do with fishing, or omens, or anything. People dream, and so what?' Gaëtan doesn't mean to sound impatient.

'I dreamt but I don't want to tell you about the dream,' says

Robert, as if this will explain. Jean-Paul is still smirking at him and he realises that he has missed any chance of sympathy. He hadn't meant to say anything, it just came out.

Gaëtan looks up into Robert's face.

'You better keep your dreams to yourself, Bobo,' he says. 'People are better off keeping their dreams to themselves.'

Fifteen

Not only did Henri have useful contacts in Bourail, he managed to land Catherine a job. A friend of his at the Chambre de Commerce was looking for an English teacher for their classes, starting that same week. The *professeur* who had been engaged had developed acute appendicitis requiring surgery and would be absent for three weeks. Would Catherine be interested to start the group? There were a dozen or more students enrolled and ready to begin. No, it didn't matter that she had never taught English, there was a course book. All they needed was a facilitator, preferably English-speaking. They could help with accommodation. Could *la poken* let them know as soon as possible?

Catherine couldn't have imagined a more perfect opportunity.

The meeting room of the Chambre de Commerce was adequately lit, at least, and with the windows open she still had the sense that the velvet evening was there to be savoured despite the unknown nature of the task ahead. The overhead fans beat reassuringly, swirling up a mixture of Dior and aftershave and the scents from a range of soaps.

An aura of respectful anticipation filtered through the room as the participants waited for Catherine to open her mouth. She sensed it was uncharacteristic. Surveying the room, she took in the diverse collection of faces, some oily and tanned, others showered and freshened in the brief hour between finishing work and signing on for their first English lesson with the replacement *prof*. Would she make sense? Would they follow?

'Good evening to you all,' she started, in English. 'It's nice to be here on such a lovely evening.' In fact she might rather have been on the dusk-lit beach, escaping the stickiness of the village, dipping her toes in the limpid water. 'I'm Catherine, and I'm from Adelaide, which is in Australia, to the west of Sydney and a long way down from the Gold Coast.'

Better not to let on that she was born in France, not just yet.

A quick check of their polite but blank faces revealed she had already lost half of them. Maybe she would have to sort them out into different levels as soon as possible.

'So, who's here?' Let's see who was curious enough to enrol in a term of English in this lost little village half-way up the country and a million miles from anything she could associate with her former life.

'Would you like to introduce yourselves, yes in *English*, don't be scared, just tell me who you are and what you do, that's all. Let's start with you, Monsieur,' she finished, decisively, as she roved the room, observing them one by one avoid her eye. 'Come on, tell me your name. You must be able to remember how to say that.'

A few laughs, they were warming up a little.

'*Qui . . . moi?*' said the man, a solid, egg-headed type. The man turned to his colleagues, entreating someone to rescue him. '*Allez, Honoré,*' someone whispered.

'*Euh . . . bonjour,*' managed Honoré, his face a red balloon of embarrassment.

'Welcome to the class, Honoré. And what do you do, Honoré, apart from learning English as a hobby?'

Honoré was getting nudges and whispers while he averted his eyes, shrugged and shuffled his feet under the table.

'Tankyou,' he announced finally, after some coaching from the ranks.

The reasons for Honoré's presence left her mystified.

By the end of some twenty minutes she had established the composition of the group. Thirteen altogether. The butcher, the doctor's wife, the school inspector, the owner of the snack bar. A gendarme, the pharmacist and the secretary at the *Mairie*. Two Jean-Pierres and of course, a Jacques, the owner of the sawmill. A young Indonesian woman and a shy Melanesian woman with her daughter. Representation from no less than the entire village, whether from curiosity or boredom or even a real desire to learn English. The whole village, with their stories, their connections and liaisons. She was the outsider.

'Okay, thank you everyone, well done,' she said finally. 'Let's have a look at the course books.'

'But what brings you here, Madame, to our small town?' ventured the ruddy-faced butcher, eyes bright in anticipation of the answer. All eyes were on her.

The question seemed too familiar. She hesitated before speaking, but was interrupted anyway.

'A man, or the police, or both!' quipped Jacques, to murmurs of concordance and a few respectful nods in the direction of the gendarme.

Catherine looked through the shutters to the outline of the coconut palms, darkened against the sky.

'I needed a change.'

Silence greeted this pronouncement. Whether they understood or not, no one moved. Through the window came the only sound: the flapping of palm fronds.

She drew in her breath, aware that this answer had not satisfied them.

'I am . . . researching,' she said finally and dropped her hands.

'*Ah, non*, Madame,' enticed one of the Jean-Pierres. 'Do not disappoint us!'

His insistence took her by surprise, though it seemed good-natured enough.

'An affair, for sure,' said Jean-Pierre the second. 'It is always at the bottom of everything.'

'No, something worse than that,' interjected Jacques. 'It would have to be to come to a place like this!'

Laughter followed this assertion.

'You are not the only one, Madame, to do stupid things, if it is that, or even worse things,' said Jacques. His eyes had turned indiscreetly to the secretary. All eyes followed. The woman flushed and feigned ignorance.

'Eh, that's enough, Jacques,' said the pharmacist. '*Your* life is hardly an example.'

'And you! You can talk!'

'I don't think anyone is much of an example, here,' said Marie-Claude, the doctor's wife. 'Let's get on with the lesson.'

'I think also that we should please remember who is here,' said the Indonesian woman firmly. 'We do have some young people present.' All eyes then turned to the young Melanesian girl, who dropped her eyes in embarrassment.

'Perhaps you should see who she hangs out with after school,' said the secretary, under her breath, loud enough for Catherine to hear. 'I'm only warning,' she added quickly to the glares of the other women.

They had degenerated into very rapid French but Catherine could pick up the threads of the discussion. It was like a strong-smelling verbal fracas, a soup of old vegetables thrown into a pot and stirred.

She tried to catch their attention by clearing her throat, thankful at least that her own story had been dropped.

'Let's turn to page five.'

No one moved.

'Tell us, Madame, what brings you here? It can be nothing too terrible.'

Catherine closed the book and surveyed the room.

'I'm hoping to find . . . a member of my family.'

No further quips about lovers or affairs. Family, it seemed, was untouchable.

'What name?'

'Georges Ransan is his name. My father.'

The words surprised Catherine as they tumbled out, as if from the mouth of someone else.

'There was Georges, the *instit* at the school.'

'I knew a Georges once, worked at the sawmill.'

'Was there a Georges the dentist, I think, only stayed a while, went back to France?'

'My father worked at the mines,' she said. 'At least, I found out he was at Tiébaghi, and then Poro.'

'Ah, but they closed, at Tiébaghi, yes, he might have moved on to Poro or Kouaoua.'

'Madame, why don't you come to the *Mairie*?' said the secretary. 'We have all the local records there.'

'Yes, but he wasn't born here, so I don't think that will help. We spent time here when I was only a toddler. Then, well, we were separated.'

'Madame, you should come to the medical clinic,' offered Marie-Claude. 'My husband knows everyone in the region and has just about seen them all through the clinic for one reason or another. He might be able to help.'

This offer gave way to a round of applause. It certainly seemed like the best lead.

'Either that or come my way,' said the gendarme. 'I've seen just about everyone too!'

More laughter.

'Well, I'd appreciate that very much,' said Catherine. The lesson had ended well, the group somehow united in support for her problem, whatever the level of their own interpersonal jousting.

She left feeling uplifted and intrigued by their frankness. Wondering, too, if by the next lesson they would ever get on to some language study.

———~⌒

Robert has never stood up to Dominique before.

'I could do the rodeo. I've had enough practice.'

'It's stupid. Too dangerous.'

'But have you seen me?'

'No. I don't want to. I don't want you to. You're not tough like those others – they've had years of practice. You're too young.'

'So?'

'Robert, I'm not happy. You have to be an adult anyway.'

'Nobody cares. They only care how good you are.'

'What did Gaëtan say?'

'He didn't say anything. He just shrugged.'

'As usual.'

'Which means he didn't say no.'

'Which means he didn't say yes. Robert, usually you listen to reason.'

'Frédéric is going to give it a go.'

'Well, you're not Frédéric.'

'But I've had more chance to practise than him. If he can go in it I should be able to. I'm better than him.'

'Robert, I'm not happy. I'm not even sure it will take place. But in any event, I'm not happy.'

'I'll win, you'll see. That'll make you happy. That'll make him happy.'

Dominique tosses Robert's report card across the table.

'What's going on? You're hardly passing.'

Robert shrugs.

'You were coming top of history. I can't understand.' Underneath she does, really, understand. She wants Robert to articulate it, to be sure.

'I'm not that interested in the history of France.'

'It's not just French history. It's not just the geography of France.'

'Do you want to see what I've been learning?' challenges Robert. 'I've been studying Charlemagne. I know all about "our" ancestors, the Gauls. I've learnt about the Romans and Roman colonisation. I can recite the names of all the rivers of France, off by heart. I know all about the production of wheat; have you ever seen a field of wheat? About the climate in the Rhône valley. Is that what you think I should learn?'

'It's part of your heritage, too. Some of my ancestors were from the Rhône valley.'

'Yes, and my heritage? Which heritage do you mean? On my father's side? Why should I care about where he was from? Nobody knows anything about him.'

'Well, you know as much as we do. We know – well, we think he was French.'

'White, you mean. You only know that he was white.'

It is true she has told him only what she has surmised. She knows also that it is not her assumptions that he needs to hear now, again. But she persists, because at least it is a conversation of sorts, the machinery of which has lately ceased at the family table.

'What about literature? *Le Petit Prince*? I thought you loved it. I thought you wanted to go on.'

Robert shrugs again.

'Robert, this is your future. You need to realise that. You can do something with your life, or you can just stay here, like us, and grow old, doing what? We were hoping . . .'

'*You* were hoping?'

'Your father and I were hoping – '

'You mean *you*. Gaëtan doesn't care. He doesn't want me to go down to Nouméa.'

'He does really, he just doesn't say what he thinks, you should know that by now. Of course he thinks it would be better to go on.' In her mind she knows this is not really true, and is equally certain that Robert knows she is lying. But suddenly she wants to present a united front; it is the weakest best she can do, to try to convince him.

Robert doesn't answer. Perhaps there isn't an answer, thinks Dominique. Perhaps there really isn't an answer.

'Well, Robert, it is up to you. With these marks I don't think you'll make it anyway. Is that really what you want?'

'It's a bad time to go anyway,' says Robert. 'Gaëtan needs me here. *You* don't even feel safe here now.'

This time Dominique doesn't answer. He is right. All three boys, for all the grief they have caused them, have seemed united in this singular, simple act of loyalty: to protect the farm.

Should she ruffle his hair? Should she try to hug him, tell him she is at once disappointed, relieved, angry, reassured, frustrated, fearful, compromised? That she could see another life for him, beyond the town, beyond his origins, other doors into other worlds? Does she have the right to alter his unfolding destiny as you might try to offset a ship from its course? Though perhaps she has no right, could she ever tell him how much she would grieve the loss of potential, should he choose to follow Gaëtan's path, or even take the road back to his *tribu*? Can she tell him these things? She looks at his face, that beleaguered face barely settled into his tense half-white, half-black skin and tries to imagine, tries to feel as he does in it. She shakes her head, finding she can't, and turns to go. The report card lies before them on the table.

Was it a dream? Robert stands on the bank, his back turned to Gaëtan. The net lies beside the tackle bag, as yet unrolled, a silent symbol of defiance. The day should be perfect; the stillness of everything, the brilliance of the sun on unruffled waters, Gaëtan's unmoving shape, taking in a slow cigarette, just behind the mangroves. Silence, unbroken even by the occasional slap of water against the banks. Something, if he tries to grasp it, should be perfect about the day, the time, the timelessness, the man he has suddenly seen as old.

But no, he wants to scream at the furious sun and to slash the sea and the sky into jagged strips, to squeeze the blood dripping red from its stubborn blue, to smear it over the horizon. He wants to tear the net and hurl it into the black river.

And all this he should contain, as the old man contains his patience, waiting for the moment to fish. He should see the river as perfectly blue, reflecting the sky, the water gently lapping.

Fury boils under his rib bones and claps inside his head. It won't stop, it beats more strongly and faster than he can control, like a record played at the wrong speed. He cannot let the old man see his pain. Only the anger.

The net lies between them and he scowls out to the vast, deep universe.

Sixteen

The medical clinic was housed in one of the original buildings of Bourail, dating from the penal settlement of 1867. The high ceilings were insulated against the heat and the flagstone under Catherine's feet was cool and solid. The doctor's wife had offered her the invitation but she felt uneasy about it. He was surely a busy man. She watched the criss-crossing between rooms. One or two doctors at most and a few nurses moving purposefully, eyes down, oblivious to her presence. Patients, depending on their ailments, moving more slowly. She found a bench in the corridor and sat down to wait for what she anticipated might be a long time, feeling certain she would have to remind the admissions clerk of her mission.

Thinking she had identified the right doctor, she stood to obstruct his path, knowing of no other means of attracting his attention.

The doctor jumped back and looked her in the face, confused by this unfamiliar initiative from a stranger.

'Dr Bernard? I'm very sorry to interrupt you, but I was told you would be able to see me briefly. Catherine Piron.' She extended her hand.

'But – I do not know you, Madame.' The doctor frowned.

'I know,' she said hastily. 'Your wife suggested I call in. I'm looking for any information about my lost father, Georges Ransan, and she thought you might – '

To her relief, Dr Bernard placed a hand on her shoulder, ushering her forward to a free room.

'*Oui, mais oui, bien sûr!* Come. I have five minutes.'

'Thank you. I'd appreciate any information. We . . . we were at Poro a week ago and I met a nurse there who knew him. She said he had been sent to Bourail after a fight or something.'

'Yes, yes, look, why don't you come to our house for dinner? My wife tells me you are a good teacher and we have a lot of interest in Australia. Come, and I will tell you what I remember, which is not very much, I warn you.'

Catherine was warmed by his generosity. On the surface people might seem wary, but what they needed was to place people according to some formula, and nationality seemed to be an acceptable one. That barrier passed, they were openly welcoming. Her Australian nationality seemed to be considered a curiosity, a little exotic in some ways. She couldn't place Dr Bernard – perhaps he was from France, but perhaps not.

'I'd love to, thank you. Can I bring something?'

He waved her on. It wasn't done.

Dinner was a mid-week seafood treat. Deciding to impress the new *professeur*, Marie-Claude had prepared mud crabs; you just pay the kids, she told Catherine, to catch them down in the mangroves. Freshly boiled, their enormous, fire-red claws were displayed victoriously atop a mound of lettuce. Bowls of mustard dressing and aioli were set beside, and bright yellow lemons completed the platter. For once Catherine did not have to claw out her own crab meat; she was given, as must be the custom for guests, the best, most delicate parts, already cracked, the tumbling sweet meat unimaginably fresh.

Although she was anxious for news she knew it would not be until after dessert – *flan au coco* – and short black coffees that the doctor would tell his story.

'So you find out this Georges Ransan was your father. An amazing discovery, at your age.' He smiled and Marie-Claude took his hand, looking on sympathetically.

'Yes, I have a whole lifetime to catch up on, now.'

'Well, I'll tell you what I know. We did admit Georges here, your nurse was correct. It was a long time ago, must have been back in sixty-nine or seventy. I remember him because – well I'll tell you – it was not long after we arrived here, but before I went back to France to train in obstetrics. And yes, I've been here ever since. Stoic, *n'est-ce pas?*'

Catherine smiled politely.

'Georges wasn't in good shape when they sent him over. I remember because he nearly lost his eye. He'd been in a fight and must have had a bottle smashed over his head. I'm sorry if this is upsetting. Shall I go on?'

'Please, yes.'

'Anyway, I managed to get the shards out safely and he was all right.'

'Who else was involved?'

'Well, it caused quite a stir at the time because it was, they thought, the *chef*, you know, of the Néwé *tribu* on the east coast, who appeared to be responsible for the assault. It was unusual because it was not the sort of thing this man would usually do. Some others were involved as well, so we never found out who was really responsible. But I can tell you one thing for sure, there was no alcohol involved. I would have smelt it on them, but no. It must have been something personal.'

'Did you treat the other man, the *chef*?'

'No, he stayed in Poro. He wasn't as badly hurt.'

'What do you think it was about then, I wonder?'

'The rumour was – and this is only rumour – people said Georges was, how shall we say – having a relationship with the *chef*'s niece. It wasn't accepted, you know, in those times, a white man, and especially not one so much older, with a young girl.'

He looked up to see Catherine tightening her hands into a ball and leaning forward tensely on the sofa.

'I'm sorry again if this is painful.'

'No, no – please go on.'

'I didn't know Georges very well but I would say, if it's of any reassurance, that he wasn't a bad sort. I'm not just saying that because you're here, because that is what you want to hear. I know because he was, how can I put it, a very appreciative man. He stayed here in the clinic for a week or so after I had stitched him up, so we got to have a few conversations. He had spent time in Australia, you know, and I was interested in Australia. He was, in a way, a little more, how shall we say, open-minded. More broadly travelled, I suppose, than some of his workmates. He knew other things, other worlds.'

Catherine was silent for a moment. Not because she had no questions, but because she was struck by the irony of her father being so close to her, perhaps, in her lifetime. The idea that she might have bumped into him at Circular Quay without knowing was intriguing and, in a faint way, comforting.

'What was he doing in Australia? Was it Sydney? Brisbane?'

'Labouring, I think. Sugar cane in Queensland, building in Sydney. He had moved around.'

Catherine made some quick calculations. 1970. The article about her – he must have kept it from his time in Sydney – though that was later, 1976. Perhaps he had gone back and forth, that's what Louise said. An itinerant. It fitted.

She shifted her position on the sofa. 'The *tribu* – can anyone visit?

'Well, I'm not so sure about that,' Marie-Claude intervened. 'You might not – I hate to disappoint you – but you might not be very welcome.'

'*Chérie*, things can change,' said her husband, patting her on the knee.

'If it were possible, I would like to meet the young woman,' continued Catherine, undeterred. 'She'd be middle-aged now, my age even.'

'I suppose you could try,' said Marie-Claude. 'You could ask Adèle, you know, the Melanesian woman in our class. She might have a way of organising an invitation.'

'I wonder what her name was.'

'The young girl? I couldn't tell you that,' said the doctor. 'It was only rumour anyway. I try not to partake of it. I have to respect confidentiality. Except, of course, in this case, I suppose. But this is different.'

'Well, thank you, I appreciate you being able to speak so openly.'

'That's all I can tell you, Catherine. I'm sure you'll have more questions. Ghislaine, our nurse here may be able to help too. She's been around for a long time. She might remember Georges.'

The conversation turned to Catherine's life in Australia, her childhood in France and the cultural threads they shared. Catherine was surprised to find herself shedding the formality of her 'stranger skin'; by the end of the evening it was as if she had shared a meal with old friends.

'It's been a lovely evening, thank you,' she said, shaking hands on the verandah. She stepped between the pots of cascading ferns, through a rainforest of creepers and climbers. The warmth of the air around her felt exactly the same as the warmth of her body, so that she wasn't even sure she was moving through it, or where her limbs ended and the air began. It gave her a feeling of weightlessness, as if she were drunk, though she was sure she hadn't had more than a few glasses of Dr Bernard's *St Emilion*. Or had she? Now she tried to count she couldn't remember.

'*Chéri*, walk her to her apartment,' she heard Marie-Claude whisper to her husband, as Catherine tripped, doltishly, down the step onto the driveway. 'I'll see you tomorrow in class, Catherine. *Bonsoir.*'

It is brilliant midday along the *quai* and the sun glares blindingly out from the sea. A Melanesian woman, in her middle years and in a hurry, is moving along, stumbling a little on the footpath edges where it crumbles into nothing. She walks purposefully, in apparent concentration on her mission. Her broad cushioned hips wobble in a rolling movement, side to side like swirling water seen through a porthole. At the moment she looks down to her belongings she nearly bumps into a lean young man just exiting a bar on the street. Her bag falls to the ground in the collision and she bends to retrieve it. The man succeeds in sweeping it up before she can grab it, nearly dropping his cigarette, and presents it to her. They look at one another fully in the face. The woman starts in surprise and the man, too, seems startled.

'It is you?' says the woman. 'Monsieur Georges?' She looks into his face, at his light-brown hair.

The man lowers his head and retreats a step. The woman stays where she is, but straightens. The man turns to face the sea, one hand scratching his neck, the other flicking cigarette ash. He squints in the sunlight.

'It is you,' she repeats. 'You are back? Where are you living?'

Still the man says nothing. He glances away, as if he can't even look the woman in the eyes. He pinches his cigarette butt and tosses it over his shoulder, shoves his hands into his pockets, hunches over. His foot starts to swing in the gutter. He toys with a broken bottle, a discarded cigarette packet, debris from the bar. When he finally turns to her his face is contorted.

The woman in turn lifts an open palm to him. Her gesture signals *Stop, stop. Easy. Calm.*

'Look, Monsieur, you are wasting to nothing,' says the woman. 'What are you eating?'

The man doesn't respond. He looks back into the gutter. Shame, perhaps, or anger, it is impossible to tell.

'Where are you living? I'll come around. Let me help, Monsieur.'

'I have to get out,' he replies eventually.

'Let me help,' she repeats. 'Where shall I come?'

'I'm leaving tomorrow,' he says. 'To Poro. Think I can get work there.'

'I'll clean it out, Monsieur,' she says. 'Your place. Let me sort it out.'

The man turns to face her now, moves as if he is about to embrace her, yet something holds him back.

'Louise . . .' He is about to say something, but can't. He drops his hands, his head. 'Louise,' is all he can say. Then 'rue Pasteur, number eleven.'

'Rue Pasteur,' Louise repeats. 'I'll get someone to take me. Leave it to me, Monsieur.'

The man's face is breaking up. He still can't look at her, stares down at his feet. He pulls away, about to leave.

'You look after yourself then, Monsieur Georges,' she says.

Georges doesn't reply, turns, disappears, hunched, hands in pockets, down the street.

Seventeen

Ghislaine didn't remember a Georges. No, not even after Dr Bernard's story. Perhaps the incident had occurred before she had taken up her post in 1970. That was in July. July the fifteenth, she remembered, straight after *la fête nationale*, and three weeks after her sister had lost her baby.

'Which *tribu* did the doctor say?' she queried. 'Maybe someone here will know someone.'

'Néwé,' said Catherine. 'Over on the east coast.'

'Néwé?' repeated Ghislaine. 'Oh, that's curious.'

'Why, do you know anyone from Néwé?'

'Not personally. Not directly I mean. But it's funny you should mention it. I was just thinking of, well, just coincidence but I was just thinking of them the other day.'

'A coincidence?'

'No, no, nothing to do with your search. But we had a young girl – very sad it was – we had a young girl from that *tribu* who died here, just after I arrived. I'll never forget it.'

Catherine was disappointed by the lack of information about Georges but let Ghislaine's story distract her. 'Was she sent here ill?'

'No, she was – found dead on the riverbank. She had just given birth . . . we never knew . . .'

'Died in childbirth – alone. How terrible.'

'Anyway, just a coincidence that she was from the same *tribu* as the one Dr Bernard mentioned.'

'Ghislaine, can you remember how old she was? And her name?'

'Clémentine,' came the reply, 'which we found out later. They couldn't identify her for a while. Beautiful girl, so sad. She was only about sixteen, at a guess. We never really got all the facts.' Ghislaine sighed heavily. 'It was a tragic case. I was the one who – '

'Dr Bernard never said anything about a young girl coming from Néwé, the same *tribu*,' interrupted Catherine.

Ghislaine frowned. 'I don't think he was here, actually, when I started at this clinic. In fact, no, he definitely wasn't. He was back in France doing his obstetrics training or – '

'The baby,' said Catherine. 'What happened to the baby?'

'The baby survived. I looked after him – it was a boy – in those first few weeks before they found him a home. Are you all right?'

'Ghislaine,' said Catherine. 'What did he look like – the baby?'

'He had fine gold hair and skin the colour of café au lait,' said Ghislaine, meeting Catherine's eyes. 'He was beautiful. I called him Robert.'

Catherine called from a public phone outside the post office but the machine kept swallowing her coins and cutting her off.

'*Le Journal*, yes, please, can I speak with Henri? It is urgent, don't ask me to *patientez* again, *please!*'

Finally she had Henri on the line.

'I think I've found out something really important. Can you hear me?'

'Just.'

'I think – I think, but I'm not sure – that I may have a brother, a half-brother I mean.'

No response.

'Can you hear me? Are you still there?'

'Of course, of course. I told you that you would be related to half the country!'

'Not funny. Anyway, it's only a guess at this stage.'

'A half-brother. Have you met him? How do you know?'

'It's the story I've pieced together from everyone I've met. The doctor remembered Georges when he came in after a fight. He said rumour had it Georges was having a relationship with a young Melanesian girl. The nurse, Ghislaine, remembered a girl – from the same *tribu* as the one near where Georges worked – who died in childbirth. Ghislaine didn't ever know about Georges, you see, because he must have been there before she took her position, so they never connected the two stories. But somewhere out there is the baby – who must be in his mid-twenties by now – who could be my half-brother! Isn't that amazing?'

Again, a long pause.

'Henri, are you following me?'

'Well, I suppose it is possible. But how do you know for sure?'

'I don't. But Ghislaine has told me enough that I suspect it must have been the girl he was having a relationship with. She was young and alone, there must have been a reason for that. Maybe she was ashamed of her pregnancy and ran away. She died all alone, not even in the clinic. They found her on the riverbank.'

'Have you checked the records? They must have some at the *Mairie*.'

'Well, this is the wonderful thing about teaching the English class – everyone in the village is there. So I was able to check the records. And there is an entry for a Robert Paul Jacques, born in July 1970. If it is him, he was given three Christian names, as I was told they do with orphaned children.'

'So what happened to him? It's strange that he was not returned to the *tribu*.' Henri's voice drifted off.

'Ghislaine was vague about where he ended up. Something about a social worker and some foster families and it not working out. But she thought I might be able to find the social worker who dealt with it all. Ghislaine thinks she could be in Nouméa now.'

'What is her name?'

'Céline, Céline Jacob.'

Another pause while Catherine waited for Henri to announce whether he knew her or not.

'I'll ask around. So – what about Georges?'

'Yes, Georges. No one seems to know where he's disappeared. He's not in Poro. He's not in Nouméa. He's not here. Someone suggested the mines in Kouaoua.'

'Catherine, you should check death records as well.'

'I know. I did, while I was at the *Mairie*. Nothing there.'

Abruptly she was cut off. She fumbled for her purse, finding she had no small change. *Merde.*

As she stepped out of the booth in frustration she couldn't mistake Honoré, waddling up the steps to the post office and perhaps, now, to her rescue. He might struggle with new concepts but Honoré proved to be most obliging. In a moment the line was re-established. Too late. Henri was not to be found at his desk.

'Could you let him know I called?' she said, annoyed at having to speak to Martine again. 'Tell him I'll try again later today.'

'I'll pass it on, Madame.'

Catherine doubted very much that she would.

It is late morning when they knock on the door at Rosina's house, two tall gendarmes in khaki uniform. Rosina has been in charge of the kids, her mother has walked into the village to do the shopping. Robert is showing her a few chords on her father's guitar. At first when Rosina sees the officers she thinks her little brother is in trouble again – he was caught lighting fires last week.

'Is your father home?'

'No, he's out fishing.'

'So, are you – ?'

'I'm Rosina. I'm the eldest in the family – well, apart from my older brother – he's with my father.'

Robert, coming up behind, touches her elbow. 'Ask them in,' he whispers.

'Why . . . what do you want?' she says, not moving.

Still standing at the door, the officer pauses before speaking. 'You are, Monsieur?' he says, inclining his head.

'Robert Naudin. I'm a family friend.'

'There's been an accident,' says the officer.

'An accident.' Rosina frames it as a statement.

'There's been a fatal accident.'

Robert steps forward, takes Rosina's shoulder. 'Come in, please, come in,' he says.

The men step politely past Rosina, who remains standing, stunned, in the frame of the door. She doesn't turn until Robert pulls her hand. 'Come on, come and sit down.'

It takes a few moments for the men to settle themselves on the chairs.

'Rosina, I'm afraid there's not an easy way to say this. Maeva – that is your mother's name?'

'My mother, yes. She's out shopping. She shouldn't be much longer.'

'I'm sorry, Rosina. She's been hit by a car.'

'She couldn't have been. She only left an hour ago.'

'I'm afraid, Rosina, she was hit at about ten-thirty, about forty-five minutes ago, and . . . I'm sorry to have to tell you this, but she succumbed to her injuries.'

'What are you saying?' says Rosina slowly.

'She died instantly. I'm very sorry.'

Rosina's sister appears at the doorway to the sunroom, eyes wide with questions. Robert tries to wave her away.

Rosina stares at her sister and then turns back to the officer. 'She only left an hour ago. She was here an hour ago. It's – it's only eleven thirty in the morning.'

'I'm terribly sorry, Mademoiselle. It's a terrible thing. What happened was – she was walking along the side of the road and, unfortunately, a car came around the bend too quickly and – '

'I don't know what you're saying,' says Rosina. 'You must have the wrong person. My mother was only here an hour ago.'

'Yes, I understand,' says the officer, and addresses the next words almost under his breath to Robert, who has understood. 'We'll have to return, sir. She is in shock. Are you able to stay with her? I don't suppose you know where Rosina's father is fishing?'

'Straight out in the bay, Monsieur,' replies Robert. 'Is it true, is it not a nightmare? What happened again?'

'It appears she was hit by a car driving too fast around the bend. Those responsible have been apprehended. They are in fact all there still at the scene, but I advise,' and he drops his voice, 'you don't go there, sir. I advise you to stay here until we are able to locate Monsieur Tamanu.'

'Who was it? Who did this?' says Robert.

'I'm not at liberty to disclose that at this point. I'm sorry, sir, but it appears to be an accident. Of course, there'll be an enquiry.

It was our job to inform the family. The body of Madame Tamanu is at the dispensary. I'm terribly sorry, sir. It's a most terrible thing. Is there any other family close? Brothers, sisters?'

'I – I can ring them. They're a little way – down the coast,' coughs Robert, his mind a sickening blank as to what he will say.

'We'll arrange for them to be informed, sir. It's better. You stay here, if you wouldn't mind, sir, the young mademoiselle is in shock now. She may need to go up to the dispensary but I advise you to stay here until her father can be contacted.'

The officer can see Robert's ability to comprehend any more information has reached its limit. He has seen this before. Too many times. The faraway expression of shock, the struggle to grasp.

'We'll leave you then, sir, and if you could just give me those addresses.'

'What addresses?'

'Of your, rather Mademoiselle's relatives . . .'

'Oh, yes, of course. I'll have to ask her.'

After they have gone Robert turns back to Rosina, not sure at first, from her grey expression of denial, whether she will push him away. But she sinks into him with a howl of pain so intense that he feels he is touching a moment in time, knows that life from now can only turn irrevocably, and that they are at the pinpoint between future and past, between the future unknown and their wrenched childhoods.

Eighteen

The days passed in a blur. Soon Catherine recognised almost every car driving through the village. She settled into a kind of time-rich lull, punctuated by brief cognitive effort to prepare her classes. Her students made her feel at home, and the challenge of explaining the definite article – lesson one of her course – to Honoré provided a diversion from the intensity of her search. After the movement of those first few weeks in Nouméa it was a relief to have no other accounts to render, and she realised that what she needed more than anything else was a holiday.

The beaches were quiet during the day and weekends brought only a few tourists, backpackers or the occasional Japanese couple, to the snorkelling beach of Poe. Where previously she had never much liked the solitude of an isolated beach she found now she relished the easy hours sitting, watching, thinking. She declined an invitation to go waterskiing one weekend, not out of any apprehension about boats or fear of ridicule – though both were valid – but because she needed time. Time to understand the new revelations about her father's life. For the first time in a long while it was a need, not a burden to be on her own.

She kept in touch with Louise, though with difficulty. Louise didn't have a telephone, nor did she read; Catherine knew it would be Hélène who would have to read and compose their correspondence. Return mail seemed slow to Catherine; short polite messages, giving abbreviated detail of what Louise remembered about Georges, congratulating her on her discoveries, encouraging her to continue her search. For Catherine it did not quite fill in the picture and she knew she would have to wait until her return to Nouméa to glean more.

In another way, though, she was content. Perhaps in her quieter moments of reflection she might admit to not being ready for too much detail; in fact not ready at all to dismantle any of her illusions about Georges.

The market, held at the dusty end of the main road each Saturday morning, was a high point in the life of the village, a diversion from the unruffled monotony of a quiet rural town. On weekdays people went about their business, stopped to talk in the street, collected their mail from the post office boxes, paid their bills, took siestas after lunch and re-emerged in the early afternoon to start a similar routine.

But the market had a different face. People came from further afield to sell their produce; corn and guavas and chokos, yams and taros, coconuts and small sweet pineapples, carrots and onions and huge green hands of bananas. Great brown mud crabs glistened on the benches, pincers bound with black string.

Something here was different from other markets Catherine had experienced in other countries. It was quiet. It didn't bustle as she might have expected. Nobody haggled, nobody called out; people spoke in soft tones; their words running over like small whirring motors, here and there a drift of dialect, perhaps a native tongue. One of the women, right in the middle of the

mostly Melanesian stallholders, looked as if she had been trans-
planted direct from the fishing markets of Brittany. White fleshy
arms squashed into her easy chair, she sat, planted behind jars
of home-made pickles and jams, brilliant red chillies, mustard
concoctions, spicy purple cabbage.

Catherine spotted the Melanesian woman, Adèle, from her
class, but felt unsure about approaching her, sitting as she was
with a group of women. Adèle looked up, then quickly back
down again in a way Catherine was starting to recognise as
the reserve which separated their cultures, the self-consciousness
of the movement from formality to familiarity. Then Adèle raised
her eyebrows and gave a backwards toss of her head in a signal
that Catherine guessed to mean, it's okay, come over here.

As Catherine approached, Adèle moved herself a little apart
from the other women, who continued talking.

'Madame,' she said, softly. 'I knew a Georges once.' She was
shy of looking at Catherine in the eye. 'He was the friend of
my friend who died.'

'She was a young woman, your friend?' said Catherine.

'Clémentine was her name. From our *tribu*, though I don't
stay there any more. She was with Georges. The men weren't
happy about it. They had a fight and we never saw Georges again.'

'Go on,' said Catherine. 'Please go on.'

'Clémentine ran away.'

Catherine waited for her to continue.

'I never saw her again, Madame, alive.' Adèle was looking into
the dirt. 'She died, near here in Bourail they found her. They found
her on the riverbank, she can't have got to the clinic.'

Catherine shook her head.

'And you think that Georges, her friend, may have been my
father?'

'Madame,' said Adèle. 'Clémentine was pregnant when she

ran away. Nobody knew but me. It must have been George's baby. The boy came back to the *tribu* one time, he traced her back. I see the girls from Néwé still. They told me he came.'

Catherine said nothing, disturbed by questions. Why had it been so secret? And the boy, where was he now?

Adèle shrugged, as if reading her mind. 'The boy grew up with some whites, up the coast, don't know who they are. It was hard for him to go back to Néwé. Two different worlds.'

'Up the coast?'

'Poindimié or Hienghène, by there. Don't know their name. But there's not too many left, since *les événements*.'

'Oh?'

'Most of them moved back down to Nouméa. Our land, you know.'

Catherine nodded. 'Did you know Georges?'

Adèle thought before replying. 'I remember he made us laugh. He was different. It wasn't usual for – you know – whites like him to hang around the *tribu*.'

'How do you mean different?'

'He wasn't like the *broussards* from here, but not like *les z'oreilles*. Perhaps, I don't know, more like an Australian. He'd travelled a bit. He had big plans.'

'I wonder . . .' started Catherine. 'I wonder how long he knew Clementine . . .'

Adèle looked away. 'Maybe it was more than just a flirt, Madame, but you know, we were so young and he was – well, getting on. It wasn't looked on too well. Especially not by the *tribu*, the men, you know.'

'I think it must have been him, you know, Adèle,' said Catherine. 'You've helped me piece together the story. Everyone had just a small part of it. I wonder why they fostered the baby out.'

'Protection, maybe. Don't know. Worried about the clan, her brothers, uncles, her father. I was young, too, at the time. I didn't know whether I should have – '

'I found out that the nurse called the baby Robert,' Catherine interrupted, saving Adèle the discomfort. 'You don't know where he is now?'

'No, but try by Poindimié. I think that was the nearest town to where his foster family lived. Or Hienghène. Go and ask. Someone will know.'

'Thank you, Adèle. Thank you.'

With no phone in her apartment she found herself having to journey to the post office to call Henri. She wondered if he had been able to track down the social worker who had fostered out Robert. Calling him at *Le Journal* was irritating, since she always had to go through Martine, who, it seemed to Catherine, would exercise right of veto depending on her mood.

But today Martine was feeling magnanimous.

'Of course, Madame, one moment.'

And in an instant he was there, the familiar sound of papers shuffling in the background, the distant, distracted voice. And today he had news.

'I've found the social worker. She lives in France now.'

'Oh.'

'But wait. She's actually here in Nouméa, on holiday. She's a friend of a friend of Martine's. Martine remembered the name.'

'Oh.'

'What do you mean "oh" again?'

'Nothing.'

'Do you want me to get Martine to organise something?'

'No – well, yes – well, I don't know,' blurted Catherine. 'How long is she here? What do you think?'

'I don't know how much longer she's here. Do you want me to tell you what to do?'

Catherine bit her lip. Yes, it was stupid, but she did. She didn't know the etiquette, or what unknowns might be uncovered in the equation. It felt intrusive.

'Sorry, I was thinking about the best way of approaching her. Maybe I should write to her first.'

'You could. But you might run out of time.'

He was busy, she could tell.

'Could I have her hotel, I wonder, if you wouldn't mind asking –'

'Catherine,' said Henri, cutting her off. 'Come back down to Nouméa on Friday. You can take time off from your classes I'm sure. Come down and I'll arrange a meeting. I'll see you at twelve here, yes? At the office – no, at the café in the square, you know the one I mean. I have to go, *allez*, see you Friday.'

Robert has heard arguments before but never like this. Dominique's voice, at a pitch so wild and forceful he cannot be sure that it is really her.

In the black of night, in the early hours, he is abruptly awake. The sound of a truck, gears grating as it approaches, all the way up the long drive to the farmhouse. It shears to a halt, the sound of gutteral throbbing as it idles. A door slamming. Insistent beating at the kitchen door. Should he go? He is closer to the kitchen than Gaëtan.

Then he is upright, the bed sheet back and his feet on the ground. Next to his room he hears Gaëtan swearing, blundering about, a thump as feet swing to the floor, Dominique's just-woken, questioning intonation. The door wincing open. A low, staccato voice, telling – what are they are saying? He does not recognise the voices and can only gauge from Gaëtan's response that it is important, or urgent, or illicit. Footsteps inside – one, two men? Clodding this way, towards his room, no; turning, towards the outhouse, through the back door. Intercepted by a woman's voice – Dominique who must have arrived in the kitchen calling out – *shouting* in defiance, demanding: *Who? Where? Why? No*, not here, not under my roof! Not even that you have lost your own. *No! Not – under – my – roof.*

Shot down he hears, can he believe his ears? *Nine, ten, don't know how many.* Nine! Nine people are dead, somewhere, in this night. *Go!* screams Dominique. *Allez! Get out of here!* Should he appear? Gaëtan is raising his voice to hers, cursing louder, almost shouting her down. But her voice washes over at a constant volume, a rhythmic, tidal steadiness: *Not here, not under my roof. Go.*

He strains to hear. Will they go or stay? In the silence his heart-beat is too loud. He fears, suddenly, that the door will open to his room. Should he rise, should he go? Will she be all right?

More swearing, this time the blunted rasping voices of the visitors. Gaëtan's voice has gone, like a character in a radio play, his part is over. The kitchen door bangs hard; two, three people leaving. *Gaëtan as well?* No, someone, it sounds like Gaëtan, returns to the kitchen in heavy, slow steps. The fading growl of the truck.

Where is Dominique? Still at the kitchen table, still enraged, or has she comfortingly, familiarly dusted it down, returned unflinching to bed? What will pass between them, now? He strains to hear.

Nothing. No sound.

Tonight there is no wind to part the curtains. Nothing that might let in a chink, a flimsy beam of light.

There are no answers in this darkness.

In the morning, nothing is said at home. But the news is out. Nine Kanaks slain on their way home from a political meeting. The perpetrators have disappeared to the mountains. Gaëtan has his ears to the CB radio, but he knows better than to share his reaction too widely. And Robert has learnt not to provoke it.

Between the three now lies a great divide, a vast, thick wall of discord, mute and impenetrable, like nothing they have ever known.

Nineteen

Stepping off the blue bus in a sluice of perspiration, Catherine made the decision to be late for the appointment. It would take at least an hour to look as presentable as she expected Céline would be. And she was secretly pleased to be seeing Henri again. This time she would take the trouble to check into her hotel, shower and iron something.

Henri had arranged the rendezvous in town, at a little café by a pond in the centre of the Place des Cocotiers. Catherine recognised Céline even before she saw Henri, a woman coolly dressed in a linen suit and slim sandals. Even from a distance it all looked expensive. And how uncreased, Catherine thought, smoothing down her own skirt, which wasn't linen, but which, at least, was not a pair of shorts.

They shook hands formally. Céline's mouth was perfectly outlined by her lipstick; at least ten minutes to get that right. They exchanged formalities, and polite conversation, as if from a script.

'*Enchantée*, Madame.'

'*Enchantée*.'

At Catherine's invitation, Céline recounted a little about her life. She was a *métropolitaine*, born in Lyon, studied in Paris but came to New Caledonia in her early twenties, her first posting. She'd spent twelve years in the country.

'I was born in France as well,' said Catherine. 'I had the chance to go to England and then Australia as an au pair. I'm at the University of Adelaide now. Linguistics. I've been teaching English in Bourail – it's been an interesting experience!'

'*Alors,*' Henri said, turning the conversation. 'What Catherine here is seeking is information about a boy, well, a man really, who she thinks must be her half-brother. Can you help us?'

Catherine liked the 'us'. But Henri was getting to his feet. *Don't go,* she wanted to say.

'Sorry, but I have to get back. I'll leave you to it.' He winked at Catherine. 'Call me later.'

Another wave of despair washed over Catherine. Another call to Martine.

Céline took out a cigarette and sat back, inhaling, waiting for Catherine to speak.

'I am trying to find out about a boy called Robert. He was found as a newborn in Bourail in 1970. His mother died in childbirth and no one knew the father. I found a record at the *Mairie* for him – he was named Robert Paul Jacques. I'd appreciate anything you could share of what you remember.'

It all felt stiffer than Catherine had planned. She had thought it all through; no searching questions, no querying of motives, of unconventional decisions, nothing that would imply unprofessional practice. But the facts of the story stuck out to her like broken bones. Céline seemed a little uncomfortable in the telling. The story wafted across in draughts, starkly cold yet at the same time reassuring in its evocation of a life, her brother's life, and the warmth that came with the possibility of connection.

'I had to make a difficult decision. It wouldn't be the same now. The politics are different today. The safety of the child was paramount for me. And I couldn't guarantee that, for him, back in the *tribu*,' she finished, stabbing her cigarette in the ashtray. 'Not after what the girl's friend told me. If, of course, what she said was true. I had nothing else to go on.'

Catherine wondered if she was being persuaded by the timbre of Céline's voice, her crisp elocution, her perfect French.

Did you visit the tribu? she wondered. Did you ever visit to find out for yourself? How come there were no questions asked?

There was a pause during which Céline looked away. Goldfish swirled in the water, a duck dipped. Some children were scooping up the leaves and in the distance, behind the statue of someone from the glorious days of the République, she could just see the *bleu-blanc-rouge* of the French flag flapping in front of the *Mairie*.

Céline folded her hands together. Slender fingers; manicured, polished nails.

'And, do you remember the people who took him?' Catherine broke the silence. 'Their name? Where they lived?'

'Of course,' she answered. 'Of course I remember them. Naudin, that was their name. They adopted him, as he was legally an orphan. Generous people; basic, straightforward. They took him in, took him on as their own. I don't know what has become of him though, of course. I left in eighty-two. Two stints of six years, enough for me. I love it here but for me, well, it was never home. And things were becoming unsettled around the time I left. I didn't feel safe out in the country.'

'Naudin,' said Catherine. 'I suppose I could look them up.'

'Probably. There won't be very many, I shouldn't think. It is a small country.'

'I appreciate your help, Madame.' First names wouldn't have been right.

Céline extended her hand, and gave a brief cracked and unconvincing smile. Her lipstick hadn't smudged.

'I wish you all the best with your search.'

Catherine had arranged to visit Louise again after her meeting with Céline. It was good to see her again, to spend time catching up on the questions she had not felt able to ask at that first meeting. What did Georges look like? Did he ever mention my sister or me again? Or our mother? Did you feel sorry for him? Was he in trouble?

Louise's words were few and well chosen; she was the kind of woman with whom the quiet sharing of space was enough for connection. Her memories of Georges were sketchy, though perhaps she was withholding something. Catherine was touched by Louise's capacity to forgive and move on. After all, her livelihood too had been affected by his desertion.

'He was not a bad man,' Louise would repeat, perhaps more times than Catherine wanted to hear. Part of her didn't want to know any more. She was satisfied, for the moment, to keep her image of him at a safe distance, with Louise's information giving enough definition to his faintly drawn profile.

So Catherine spent the last of the afternoon, in the little house overlooking the bay, colouring a lost segment of her childhood, enjoying the old lady's serenity. Louise was touched by the idea of a half-brother; intrigued by the connection. She had puckered her eyebrows as if the name were familiar. Family was important, Louise said. She herself had lost her only daughter to cancer; had raised her grand-daughter alone on a meagre living cleaning houses and the church vestry. You had to hang on to whatever little you had, and be grateful. Catherine's eyes pricked with tears at her story. She wondered what had happened to Louise's husband or whether she'd had one. 'He died, too, a long time ago,' she replied, her eyes giving nothing away. 'And my daughter, her husband was not such a good man,' was all she would disclose.

'And so I must leave you now to your evening, Louise, I think,' said Catherine as the light dimmed in the little cottage.

'Yes, Hélène will arrive soon with supper. She works the late afternoon shift today.'

'I'll see you again soon. I have one more week in Bourail and then back here. I'm anxious to find out more now about Robert.'

'Yes.'

'See you soon, then. It was good to visit again.'

'See you soon.'

On her way back to the hotel Catherine wondered if it would be too late to call Henri. He'd said to call, hadn't he? Friday – six o'clock – he'd still be at work. She thought, with a tiny surge of anticipation, about inviting him to dinner. It was a beautiful evening. *Pourquoi pas?* If he was busy, well, it would be one way of finding out.

For once she didn't have to be transferred by Martine; another receptionist put her straight through to Henri. But he sounded distracted and her idea of inviting him to dinner vaporised in an instant.

'I found out their name,' she started.

'Whose?' he shot back.

Catherine coughed to cover her disappointment. Surely he remembered? He had organised the rendezvous for that purpose.

'The parents of the boy. Of my half-brother, I'm sure of it now.'

'Oh, well, good, but can we talk another time? I have deadlines.'

A month ago, thought Catherine, she would have engineered a hasty exit from the conversation and tortured herself for bothering him. Not any longer.

'I'll call back,' she replied. 'No – *you* call back, can you? I'll be here waiting.'

'*D' accord*,' came the reply, just as decisive. 'At seven.'

Good, she thought. Still in with a chance for dinner.

———

Gaëtan has been preoccupied with the elections. He expects them all to help; there are flyers to distribute, posters to pin up. Robert reads the blurb on the fliers and feels the creep of embarrassment on his skin, sharp stabs of indignation deepening to disgust. It follows too close on the heels of his visit to Néwé, of the fusillade in the night.

In the village the voices are mixed now. Old faces look at him differently, as if he is changed. *Do they see?* he wonders. *Can they see inside?* When he looks in the mirror his face is sallow, his skin puckered with patches of light and dark, vestiges of uneasy adolescence. His eyes move in agitation, twitch, as if he must be constantly on guard. Fear of making a careless remark. When he looks into his pupils, dark and huge, he sees himself drowning with longing for another life. The shadow of his skin fights itself, his blackness, his whiteness vying to shake off the label of *métis*, of fatherless, motherless, orphan, bastard.

'What's wrong with him?' says Gaëtan to Dominique. 'He's stopped talking. Dumb as a deaf-mute.'

Dominique says nothing at first. Then, 'You shouldn't have criticised his hair.'

'What? The rasta cut? Like a Kanak.'

'He is a Kanak.'

Gaëtan shrugs, doesn't reply.

'He wants to visit, he wants to go back to his *tribu*.'

'Well, no to that, absolutely no,' replies Gaëtan.

Dominique shrugs.

'Just to visit. I can understand it.' Of course she can understand it, in a detached, non-motherly sort of way.

'No,' repeats Gaëtan. He shakes his head.

'He belongs to them as well.'

Gaëtan will not be drawn. He stands up abruptly from the table.

'*Il faut choisir*. One has to choose, in life.'

'He's only sixteen! He's just found out about his other family. It's normal to be curious, to want to know them.'

'So he can go to them. If that's what he chooses. But he can't be both.'

Dominique contemplates this. In another time, before this time of upheaval, it might have been possible. But not now. She knows Gaëtan is right, on this last point.

'Well, you asked why he is so quiet. I'm trying to explain.'

Gaëtan shrugs again and Dominique knows he has nothing more to add.

The kitchen door bangs loudly at his departure for the sheds.

Dominique finds herself driving down the coast to the *tribu* more often than is advised, given the times. Gaëtan has refused absolutely, after that first trip. He sees her support as collusion, as an act in defiance of his political principles, of what he stands for. She claims it is purely the complication of Robert's circum-stances that has to be put to right. He has to connect with his roots, regardless of the times. She and Gaëtan have been his caretakers, have had the temporary privilege of raising him, through well-meaning but misguided errors of philosophy or bureaucracy or both.

These are not the only issues they argue about, but disagreements are considered normal for them. She has never expected unwavering peace and harmony; from her own upbringing she is more used to daily shows of fiery disagreement alternated with affection. And she is from tough stock. Her forebears were from France, among the first colonial settlers to be granted hectares of land under Gouverneur Feillet, sent to the remote far north-east of the island to establish coffee plantations, develop the land. Her great-grandmother, she has been told, rode a horse to the neighbouring *tribu*, to give birth to her grandmother.

As for peace within marriage, she knows of few other couples who enjoy it. Most of her friends are in Nouméa, begrudgingly still married to their husbands of thirty or forty years, roughly the same duration as she and Gaëtan. She, like most of her friends, has made her own life and lives it despite, not necessarily alongside, her husband. Though attitudes are changing, she accepts that this is just the way things are.

Sometimes, cleaning out the chicken coop, she pauses to consider whether her life might have been otherwise; whether her father, unusual as he was for the times, with his insistence on education, might have been right about her potential. That, in another day, in another time, she might have gone on to study, might have followed her instincts into nursing, instead of leaving school early to take a job as a veterinary aide. But mostly she does not dwell on what might have been, for here she is, with enough to keep her alive, and the country on the brink of insurrection to preoccupy her thoughts.

Conflict, wherever you look, is more or less severe, the only common thread being that it exists. Some of her friends' husbands have barely concealed affairs; mostly their wives put up with it for the sake of the children. Or have them themselves, not that there are rich pickings here *en brousse*. For herself and Gaëtan, she thinks, in her more philosophic moments, it is a combination of lack of opportunity and energy; that neither of them have much interest in complicating their lives, and there is no need for any further thought on the subject. Marriage, for all its shortfalls, is the mirror to society, and perhaps she should do her bit to preserve its sanctity in the face of the current unrest.

But lately, their disagreements have become commonplace, and it seems, increased by the tension in the country and their immediate area. There have been isolated attacks on white-owned properties throughout the country. They have been warned on more than one occasion to get off their property. Gaëtan is refusing to budge.

In the middle of this, there is Robert's desire to visit his *tribu* down the coast. At every roadblock it is Robert's face that gets them through, but she is fearful of misunderstandings.

For the moment there seem to be enough reasons for staying put. Robert is a priority for her; his education, his contact with his *tribu*. Even if these arguments put her out of favour with her husband, she finds herself determined to broker an imperfect peace between them all.

Twenty

When Catherine told Henri the surname, she thought the line had gone dead.

'Henri. Are you there? Do you know the name? Naudin. Does it mean anything to you?'

No response. Was he shuffling papers again? She strained, but could hear nothing in the background.

'Catherine, I – '

'What is it? Tell me what you know.'

'It's just that – '

'Henri, tell me.'

'Catherine, if it's the Naudins that I know of from the east coast – '

'I've looked them up in the phone book. There's no one by that name there.'

'That's right, but you'll find, perhaps closer to Nouméa – '

'There's three entries for the name in Nouméa.'

'Catherine – '

'What? You can tell me. It can't be much more surprising than anything I've found out so far.'

'There was an incident.'

'An incident?'

'Back in 1988, after the hostage crisis in Ouvéa. Before the presidential elections in France. Before *Matignon*. Where are you ringing from?'

'I'm back at the hotel. What's wrong?'

'Stay there,' said Henri. 'Don't go out.'

'I'm not going anywhere.'

'Stay, I'll come around.'

'Why can't you just tell me?'

'I'll be right around.'

They are at the fences, closing in.

The farmhouse creaks. In the night under a starless sky, sound travels along the paddock lines. Palm fronds flap, damp in the rising mist. Flap, flap. Like a moon beat, a pulse in the grey-green light.

Mosquitoes pierce the heat.

Moonlight fingers the shutters, casting the slats in green and black, sharpening at the kitchen window where the moths flit. Gaëtan sits in the square of light, his face the whorls of an oak. A glass of Bordeaux by his plate. He draws his finger along the table. Generations of family and mealtimes are polished into its grain. He brushes aside a crust of baguette, the remnants of brie.

Gaëtan is rooted to this table, this kitchen, this farm, this land. But he is weary too, of the love of it. He would, if he could, untangle himself from the memories, the taunts.

Outside on the porch, the dogs start to bark.

Gaëtan makes to rise but his boys appear. Jean-Paul and Didier, Robert behind. All armed.

'We'll go, Papy.'

The dogs strain at their chains, their barking swells in a gust.

'Watch it, boys, careful.' Now Gaëtan is on his feet.

'Papy, they'll cut the calf's tendons. We'll go.'

So dark outside, he sees only blackness and the whites of their eyes. His boys, *les gosses* he calls them, though they are young men. Should he let them go?

It is too quiet, suddenly.

Footfalls.

He hears Jean-Paul hiss to Didier: 'Go by the chicken coop, I'll stay in the porch. Bobo — go by the barn.'

The dogs whine and growl. Straining to hear, he hauls one in, crushes the muzzle shut.

Another footfall. The invaders are close, too near the house.

A wave of kerosene and the paperbarks crackle. He smells the oil of niaouli, freed by the heat.

'Boys!' he rasps. 'Don't switch on the — '

Too late. A flash of torchlight. Then, crack! A gunshot.

A body falling on earth.

'No! NO!' cries Gaëtan. Which boy? He glimpses, but can't see who it is, just a form, lit-up in the beam.

'Didier!' Gaëtan cries. 'Jean-Paul!'

'We're here,' calls Didier. There is fear in his throat. 'Where's Robert?'

Another shot.

Through the dark, through their skin. Through the soul, through the heart of a home. And another.

And another.

───෨───

Catherine's phone buzzed a short time later.

'It's Henri.'

'Shall I come down?'

'Come down, yes. We'll walk.'

'All right. You have time?'

'Of course, of course.'

'Maybe we could eat,' she dared. 'I'm hungry.'

'Maybe, maybe.'

When she arrived in the lobby Henri took her arm without a word, a little above the elbow, just as she remembered him doing on the day they met, when he had steered her over the pedestrian crossing in the Place des Cocotiers. But this time he didn't have the same casual air. He had that business-like agitation that she found so hard to read. It seemed as if he was avoiding her eye.

He said nothing as they crossed the road to the beachfront. There was a light breeze and the sea was calm again this evening. Catherine was distracted by the sight of the sun setting. The sky was darkening to deep blue, striped with bands of gold.

But what did Henri have to tell her? She didn't like the look of the frown on his face. It would be a set-back, another delay in the process.

'Catherine,' he said, walking a little ahead of her in a way she found irritating and at the same time a little exciting. He was so purposeful, so decisive about things. So unlike her.

'It's not easy, what I have to tell you,' Henri continued, looking out to the sea as they walked. 'This brother – half-brother, you think, of yours. Naudin. Robert.'

'Yes. I'm sure it must be, the facts all add up.'

'A young man called Robert Naudin was shot, killed during a farm invasion.' He turned to her now, stopping her in mid-stride and placing his hands on her shoulders. She squared herself, faced him, lifted her chin. The light was fading fast and she couldn't see his expression clearly.

'What?'

'Listen. It happened in 1988. The country was thrown into turmoil. It all started again, like 1984. Loyalist families were tar-geted, houses burnt.'

'Henri, what are you saying? I don't know what you're talking about.' She was pulling away from him, jagging his wrist, hair flying over her face. She took two steps back, felt the sea and the sky and the sun swirl around her like a thick soup. The thudding in her ears was muffled. Henri raised both hands, palms open, letting her go. Then he reached into his pocket, pulled out and unfolded a piece of paper, his eyes not leaving her face.

'Look at this. It's a copy of the article from the paper. From the archives. It's all recorded, Catherine. It was definitely him.' He made a gesture with his hand, beckoning her to take it.

'No,' she could hear herself crying. 'No,' shaking her head, moving backwards. 'It wasn't him. There's a mistake. There must be.'

'Catherine . . .' he dropped his head all of a sudden. 'It's not a mistake.'

She looked as if she would turn and run without stopping. 'Take it,' Henri said. 'I'm sorry to have to tell you this. I know it's true because *I* wrote the article. I was there, after it happened.'

'What!' she cried at him now, as if *he* were an assassin, as if *he* had betrayed her.

'I'm sorry.' He shrugged, shook his head. He held the paper to her, looked away, at the space between their hands. Catherine held back. The paper dropped to the ground, cart-wheeled by a gust of air to the gutter. Neither of them moved.

'If you want to, call,' said Henri finally. 'Call me.'

She stood still as he turned, hands in pockets, watching every one of his purposeful steps away.

Two figures are huddled in the lane, or it might be three, a woman a little aside from two girls sharing a grey blanket around their shoulders. It is dawn, though the smoke has smeared the rose sky with black. The neighbours stand by, some whispering in small groups, some just standing, watching. The workers have done what they can; stopped the spread of the blaze, evacuated the nearby houses. The police have been, and the ambulance, but the woman has refused to move. She stands and stares at the burnt black bones of the house. Her house. Her face registers no expression; not pain, not fear, only the anaesthesia of shock. The two girls cling to each other under their blanket. A neighbour approaches them, wary of the woman but anxious to stem the children's sobbing.

'Come now, we'll get you some chocolate and off to school, best to keep things as normal as possible for the girls, Madame Piron. We'll find shoes and clothes, don't worry.' Gently, they lead the girls away, awaiting the sting of the woman's tongue, though it never comes.

In Marthe's hand is a box, and she grips it with the ferocity of a newborn's fist around a knuckle. For five hours, she says nothing, and, after hissing at the social workers not to touch her, she doesn't move either. Not for five hours, not until the last neighbour finally manages to lead her away, on the pretext of finding some food for the mewling kitten at her feet.

Twenty-one

Emmanuel tapped lightly on the door to room thirteen. When there was no response, he followed it with three heavier raps.

'Madame Piron? Madame Piron?'

He turned to Henri and shrugged.

'Two days now, and no sign of her, except for the tea – she ordered tea last night.'

Henri pushed him aside, gave a loud knock. 'Catherine? Are you in there? It's me, Henri.'

'Open it,' he said to Emmanuel. 'Go on.'

Emmanuel hesitated, then pulled out his bunch of keys. He clicked one in the lock, pausing and listening at each turn.

He stood back as Henri moved through the doorway.

'Catherine?'

Catherine had her back to them, apparently sleeping, the breeze from the open window ruffling the sheet over her. Henri was quick to take in the state of the room. It seemed to be in order. Her things, bar a few clothes straddling her suitcase, seemed tidy. He looked quickly to the bedside chest. Nothing disturbed, the telephone handset in its cradle, next to a glass of water, half-full. A pile of used tissues.

Henri's step had been assured but he slowed now as he walked up to the still form, as if his resolve had faded, as if the strangeness of intrusion had overtaken. He listened, observed her breathing. His hand hovered over Catherine's shoulder but stopped before touching it. He walked around to the other side of the bed and squatted down to look into her face.

'Catherine, are you all right?'

No response. Henri straightened, looked around again. Emmanuel was waiting outside the room, staring down the corridor. Henri stepped into the bathroom, glanced around. No pill bottles, nothing – sharp. Nothing unusual.

Back in her room on the floor he spotted the copy of the newspaper article, the one he brought to her just two days before. *Le Journal*, Friday, 17 December 1988. The headlines he could hardly bear to see again: Invasion. Gaëtan Naudin's property near Panié burnt, son killed, two wounded.

'Catherine, wake up.'

Still no movement. He squatted again, lifted her chin with one hand, pulled gently at a swollen eyelid with the other. This action seemed finally to stir her, and she started as if his touch were scorching. She blinked and then, recognising him, sank back, burying her face in her pillow, curling around it.

'Catherine, should I call a doctor?'

She pulled the sheet over her head.

'How long have you been like this?'

'Please . . . leave me.'

'Catherine, you're not well.'

'Go, please. I'm *all right*.'

Henri sighed, moved outside to the balcony. Emmanuel coughed outside the room.

'It's all right, Emmanuel. You can go. Thank you.'

He leant on the balustrade and looked out over the bay. It was breezy today, the windsurfers were out, zipping back and forth like tiny dragonflies skittering over the water. The roar of a motor starting up, somebody's jet-ski polluting the morning peace. Suddenly his anger welled up, swept over him in a bitter wave. You could never forget, never run away, never be that detached. No matter who you were or what you believed in. Like embers of pain, it could all flare up again, even years later. The violence of the past still hurt. No one was spared.

He returned and sat at the end of her bed, his back to her, staring at the wall.

'Catherine.'

He knew she wanted him to leave. And perhaps he just should. Maybe it had to be like this for her, for a time. It was shock, a normal reaction to loss. He stood to go, but something stopped him. If he couldn't reach her, who would? If he left, she could lie here until – well, who would come? Who would be expecting news that wouldn't arrive, letters or phone calls that would just dry up? He realised how little he knew of her life in Australia. Only that she had no family.

'Catherine. Your address book. Where is it?'

No response. This time Henri took her shoulder and shook it firmly.

'Catherine. Your book. I'm going to phone your sister. Or a friend, I don't care who. But someone.'

Her hair was all he could see now of her, still bunkered under the sheet. Perhaps she wanted to answer, but couldn't.

'Catherine, I'm going to look through your suitcase until I find your address book, and I'm going to call your sister. *D'accord?* Unless you tell me to stop.'

From under the pillow there was hardly a movement, but

he was relieved, at last, to perceive a sound like buried hiccups, finally, the shifting sands of grief.

The director of the Chambre de Commerce said they would manage without her for the remainder of her contract; the *prof* was due to return anyway the following week. Catherine explained that she had personal issues to deal with; her sister was arriving from Paris, it was all very complex, she was terribly sorry, a pity she had not been able to say goodbye to the class.

In reality the class was far from her mind. Vivi's impending arrival had thrown her into a state. She had allowed Henri to contact her sister, never believing for a moment that she would come. The thought of confronting her was too hot, too close for Catherine. The memory of Paris, Vivi's collusion, Marthe's death: all as yet unprocessed, unjourneyed; ungrieved. The abrupt news about Robert's death had been the final blow. Without counting, she thought self-pityingly, the heat and the travel. And to top it all, she must have eaten something that disagreed with her; maybe the fish. At best she forced herself to rise, gingerly, in the morning; at worst she let herself wallow in hollow, sodden depression.

Henri must have informed Louise. In those first few days before Vivi arrived, Hélène would drop her grandmother at the hotel. The old lady would shuffle slowly up to the first floor and knock lightly on Catherine's door. She'd enter, tender a bag of croissants and then sit, hardly talking, on the balcony looking out to sea. Louise could share the heavy silence with an understanding that came from within. Sorrow, disappointment; these were all a part of Louise, yet perceptible only in the crinkles around her eyes, in the trail of her slow movement, as a kind of settled, owned dignity. Through the dullness of that weekend it was Louise's companionship, her wordless presence, that kept Catherine from sinking.

And Henri. She had resisted calling him. She didn't know what to think or feel. One part of her wanted him to call, to rescue, to reassure, to help her plan the next step. But at the same time she was fearful of unleashing something she couldn't define.

She was conscious of the time slipping. What more was there to discover here? Sometime soon she knew she would have to make a decision about returning to Australia.

But he'd said to call. It was up to her, not him.

She would call. She'd call soon.

Henri didn't think he could miss Vivi from Catherine's description. The woman he spotted was wearing large dark sunglasses that he thought could have been helpfully removed to aid identification. But to be fair it was still glaringly bright in the arrivals hall, especially after the greyness of a Parisian winter.

It was surely her; Catherine had so accurately predicted the scarf and handbag, the shape of her calf muscles, the taut, scanning look of contempt.

'Madame Garnier?' he tried.

She shot him a dismissive look, perhaps mistaking him for a porter.

'Henri Boulez. I'm here on behalf of your sister, Catherine Piron. Regrettably she's not well enough to be here herself.'

'Where is she?' the woman answered, but did not wait for a reply. She took his extended hand. 'Well anyway, Monsieur, I thank you, I'm most grateful.'

Henri helped her retrieve her luggage and they made their way to the car park.

'So, tell me how she is then,' said Vivi. 'It's terrible, this business, it's truly frightful, I'm very sorry.'

'She's . . . well, she's pretty low. But now, you are here. For the morale, you know.'

Vivi mumbled something that Henri couldn't quite catch,

something to do with family and morals and support and what might be easier said than done.

'It's hot,' she complained. 'It's insufferably hot. How can anyone live here?'

There was something missing, Henri thought, in the equation. He was beginning to wonder whether his idea was really so good. His brimming gallantry was being greeted with spits and scratches. Perhaps Catherine was right about Vivi.

He thought about not opening the car door for her, relenting at the last moment.

'The air conditioning takes a moment to fire up.'

'It's so humid. I'm suffocating. I hope the hotel is air conditioned.'

'I'm not sure that Catherine has splurged on a five-star hotel, not for a long stay.'

'She wouldn't.'

'I've called a doctor,' Henri said. 'She's actually physically ill, which I think has made it worse. She's got a dose of *la gratte*.'

'What's that? Sounds like head lice or something. What else have you got to tell me?'

'You get it from eating fish that have eaten certain corals. It can be quite devastating, especially on top of everything. You should watch out, too.'

He expected her to roll her eyes or shout out 'Pah!' in disgust but to his surprise she fell silent.

'Henri, excuse me for this outburst but we are so very touched by your generosity, we can't begin to . . .'

He smiled to himself as they arrived at the toll-booth on the outskirts of Nouméa. It hadn't taken long for this façade to crack.

'Don't worry, we understand,' he reflected back, amused by the 'we'. Who was she referring to? To herself and her husband?

Or her sister? Or just Vivi alone, the impersonal, detached, 'we'. He caught her eye as they pulled up at the traffic lights. Yes, she had caught his too, fleetingly, then away. He smiled to himself.

'I know she'll be pleased to see you. I'm glad you've come.'

Catherine knocked softly on Vivi's door.

'Who is it?'

Well, who was she expecting?

'It's Catherine.'

'Come in, come in.'

She entered, hesitantly. Vivi lay corpse-like on her bed, a pareo draped over her body, her eyes banded, face covered with a mixture that resembled green yoghurt.

'Can I talk to you?'

'Finally. Of course, talk to me.'

Catherine had taken her time, it was true. Henri had – gallantly, courageously – deposited her sister at the hotel, and tactfully taken leave. Catherine had stubbornly resisted making the first move; so had Vivi. But time was passing.

'Are you comfortable like this?' asked Catherine. She glanced around the room. For a woman of impeccable physical presentation, Vivi's room looked as if the bulls of Pamplona had roared through. Garments were draped over every fixture: skirts, pants, blouses, sleeveless tops. An entire corner of the room was dedicated to lingerie: white lace *balconnets* and strapless, underwired bustières, piles of dainty triangular shaped *slips* and g-strings. The washbasin was strewn with an assortment of bottles and tubes, their image of course multiplied by the mirror, but nonetheless a tumbled array of pots of wrinkle-defying cream, atomisers, shampoos, bath salts, bars of soap, eye crayons, mascara, lipsticks. The impression was one of surfeit and wasteful excess. Yet it was her sister. This *was* Vivi.

'What do you mean, like what?' said Vivi.

'Well, aren't you in the middle of some uninterruptible beauty routine?'

'Oh this. It is a new product from the beautician. Forty minutes to go.'

Catherine stared at the floor, at the recently saturated hotel towels, soggily entwined with the bath mat. The evidence of Vivi's chaotic underworld was confronting. How curious a habit, she thought, to spend so much effort preparing oneself for nobody. Almost at the same time she wondered if she shared, despite their contrasting appearances, the same fear of loneliness – a deep, hidden fear of revealing the true self.

Eyes still covered, Vivi moved, becoming conscious of the pause.

'What is it? What do you want to talk about?'

'Maman.'

'And so finally Maman. What about Maman?'

'Well, what *did* she say? After I left.'

'After you left in such a hurry.'

'It was a shock.'

'A shock, yes. But still, you leave.'

'Yes. I left. I . . . well, you know why I left.'

'Maybe I know but I still do not understand. She *died*, Catherine. You were not even there to – '

'I know, I know, I was too angry.'

'You haven't even asked how she died!'

'Well how did she, then?'

'I'd tell you if I thought you cared!' Vivi's face was becoming excited in the exchange. A blob of green cracked apart and slid down one side of her face. '*Merde*, I must keep still.'

'Did she say anything about me? Did she say she was *sorry*?'

The mask of yoghurt was immobile for a moment. 'Sorry for what?'

'Oh!' Catherine rose, making for the door in a movement clearly perceptible to the sightless Vivi.

'Why do you run away again, Catherine?' she said. '*La fugitive.* Every time, you run. Why do you not face up to the pain, there, you are like a festering abcess, why do you not lance yourself?'

'If I do run away it's because I can't talk to you. You pretend nothing ever happened, that nobody was ever hurt by this.'

'At least you were shielded from it!'

'What good does it do to be shielded from the truth, when you find out anyway?'

'It was better. We wouldn't have been accepted.'

'Better!' snapped Catherine. 'That's what *you* thought. Having the benefit of knowing, of being able to choose what story you would believe. I didn't have that luxury!'

Vivi's mouth set in a grim line, the green caking around it. Then she sat up straight, clutching her pareo. Her eye band dropped to the ground.

'Let me wipe this muck off,' she said. 'Come, we'll take the air. I'm thirsty.'

'You can't answer me, can you?' snarled Catherine, angry at the distraction of refreshments. 'Now *you* want to run away.'

Vivi had disappeared into the ensuite. Catherine heard the taps running, water sloshing. Clothing thrown on, hastily. Not her sister's usual time frame for dressing.

'*Allons.*' Vivi strode ahead of Catherine, reaching the bottom of the stairs first. Out onto the promenade, along the beach front.

'What kind of father would abandon his wife, his two small daughters?' Vivi took up. 'He was a waste, a weakling, and look at the havoc he wreaks afterwards. How could you be curious to know more?'

'Didn't you ever dream, Vivi? *I* dreamt. I imagined my father sliding into the water, sinking into sand, disappearing into the clouds. When I tried to call his name a hand came around my mouth to stifle my words. How could *you* never have said any-thing? Didn't you ever wonder?'

'I didn't care. I *don't* care,' Vivi replied. 'Why should I care about a father who deserted us?

They arrived at the *glacerie*. Catherine watched, distractedly, as the *serveuse* handed out sorbets at the front counter, enormous multi-coloured mountains, decadent with nuts and dripping chocolate sauce. She was annoyed that her sister had stopped at such a public place. Crossly, she let Vivi order her a glass of *Perrier*.

'Perhaps he couldn't help it,' Catherine said, her voice muted. 'These days they try to help people with those problems.'

'What would be the point of that! Look what he did to our mother, left her to raise us alone!' Vivi didn't seem to care that her tone was rising. 'It wasn't like today. There wasn't any help for *her*.'

'All right for *you*.' Catherine countered quickly. 'She kept *you* with her, spitting and scratching as you always did. I was sent away.' Too late, too bad if people were looking at them.

'You weren't "sent away". She had to make a hard choice. You were chosen because you were clever! An education was worth it for you.'

'That's not true! How can you – ' Catherine stopped half-way through her sentence, registering Vivi's claim. This was new. This was a different interpretation to the one she had always believed.

'Of course it was true,' continued Vivi. 'The sisters knew what they were moulding. That's why you got the scholarship, that's why you ended up where you did.'

Catherine coughed as she swallowed her *Perrier* down the wrong way.

'How can you say that! I was just the second child – more compliant – easier to dispense with.'

'No!' shouted Vivi. The ice-cream server stopped mid-scoop, startled by Vivi's face of steaming, coiled wrath. 'No! That's not true. She had to be practical. I was difficult. I admit that. I wouldn't have survived the sisters, or at least, they wouldn't have survived me. It wasn't favouritism. How can you think that?'

'That is why I left France,' Catherine hissed. 'Why I wanted to go as far away as I could. That culture never gave me anything. Just the skin of being different, the sense of estrangement. Just a name, no – affection, no encouragement.' Even as she spoke she knew her words were tumbling out half-thought, half-formed, with no order or sense. But she couldn't stop them. 'I wanted to become English from the moment I won that scholarship, at least *somebody* recognised something about me, even if it wasn't what I valued most in myself. I became that person, do you understand, the boring academic, because there was nothing else anybody saw in me!'

'That's absurd!' Vivi cried. 'You are wild, Catherine, this is complete delirium. How could you think that about yourself?'

How indeed? It seemed to Catherine that it had coloured her whole life. It was at the root of everything.

'It doesn't matter, in the end, how I came to think it. The fact is that I *did*. I felt like nobody. And coming here – coming here – finding out that there is *no one* – not a father to speak of, not the brother I imagined might have been a link to understanding myself – there is *nothing, tu comprends*? Nothing. *I* am nothing.'

'Oh, I don't believe this conversation.' Vivi got up, glaring at the waitress who might have been trying to clear her empty cup. She gathered her bag, tossed a few coins on the table. 'People make themselves, they are not fashioned by the slippery perceptions of others.'

And, yes, it looked as if she was going to walk out, perhaps to the hotel to pack her bags and take an earlier plane back to Paris. It was not a totally implausible action.

Catherine pushed aside her chair and started to follow her sister. She didn't have to go far. She stopped as Vivi turned and fell heavily against the side of a parked car.

Catherine approached slowly, realising that for once in their lives the tears must have been true and felt, or Vivi wouldn't be trying to cover them up.

Twenty-Two

Catherine sat on the bed, gazing out beyond the balcony to the sea. She would return to Australia. Back home, back to that safe, comfortable, not-unpleasant life, as if nothing had changed. Not unpleasant, no, but a life that even more seemed so bereft of direction or purpose.

She really should talk to Vivi, try again. Had they resolved anything? Catherine was still smarting from the betrayal, the painful discoveries, the deception. Better, she thought, to avoid the topic, change the subject, play tourist, accompany her sister to boutiques, or sit in the shade on the beach and let Vivi grill her delicate European skin if she wanted to.

But as the days passed it became increasingly more difficult to reintroduce the topic, especially hard not to introduce recrimination or condemnation. In a way she was surprised that Vivi had not flounced off in a fit of pique, in the style she had come to expect, nor turned her accusing finger at Catherine's own fugitive response. To her credit Vivi had kept a calm, if tight face, reiterating only that she had exactly three more days in Nouméa, after which she was obliged – absolutely – to return to Vincent.

Three days, two. Now just tomorrow. It was up to Catherine.

Catherine glanced at her watch as she stepped on to the gangway of the small marina at the Baie de la Moselle. One o'clock. She could have been any tourist in the sun, she thought, strolling by, curious, perhaps wanting to know if any of the yachts were for charter or if anyone ran day trips. She thought she had identified the correct boat, from Henri's description. He might appear from under the sail at any moment. She strained to hear. Was that a voice, two voices? Who could it be? She realised she might be about to disturb Henri with someone. Why hadn't she thought of that? She turned to go, her courage failing her.

'*Tiens!*'

'Henri!' she exclaimed, then remembered she shouldn't sound surprised. Clearly she *wasn't* just passing by.

'What a surprise!' he said. 'Welcome to *chez moi*. You are recovered. And finally you visit.'

'Oh, I really won't stay, you're busy, I can see.' Catherine could still hear a voice faintly from inside the cabin. She was surprised to feel annoyed. Annoyed and, if she had to admit the truth, *jealous.*

'What can I do for you today, Madame?' Henri scooped up a sponge from the bucket on the small deck and continued washing the cabin windows.

'I came – I wanted to thank you, for – '

Henri looked at his watch. 'Five days later, so prompt!'

'I'm sorry. Are you – well, are you alone?'

'Me, alone? What do you think, Madame Piron?'

He looked up at her, gave her a quizzical smile. Then he took her hand, in a gesture that reminded her of that first day, yet which today felt more insistent, almost natural.

'Yes, I am alone,' he said, tugging her hand. 'The radio is, of course, good company. But there is no risk of disturbing me. As it happens I am quite happy to be disturbed just now.'

Catherine switched her gaze to the horizon, which she could have sworn had just tilted. He was drawing her to him; she resisted for an instant, but kept hold of his hand.

'Henri,' she started, too quickly. 'I've probably found out as much as I can now. I wanted to tell you that I will probably be leaving soon and – '

'I don't think so,' Henri interrupted. He still had her hand.

Catherine looked down at their interlaced fingers.

'I doubt you will be leaving so soon,' he said.

Eleven o'clock. Was it was too late to disturb Vivi? Catherine listened at the door. No sound. Had she gone out? She pulled out a scrap of paper and a pencil from her bag and scribbled a note, pushing it under the door. Softly she crept back to her own room. She'd run a bath. Then sit out on the balcony a while before turning in.

But she had no time for either. There was a tap at the door. It was Vivi.

'I'm leaving, Catherine, you know, in the morning.'

'I know.'

'I'll get a taxi. There's no coach. Only the local bus.'

'I know. I wish . . . I'm sorry, I can't take you.'

'It's fine.'

'Early tomorrow, isn't it?'

'I'll book it for five.'

'I'll come to say goodbye.'

'I'll knock if you don't.'

'How did she die, Vivi?' said Catherine abruptly.

'It was her heart.'

Catherine stood, staring at her sister.

'Are you going to ask me in?' said Vivi.

'Of course, of course.' Catherine opened the door wide. Vivi walked past her, through to the balcony. Catherine followed. 'So, her heart.'

'It gave way, you could say,' said Vivi. She looked out to the water. 'Oh.'

Another pause.

'There was no letter?'

'No. There is still the succession of course. Things to sort out in Paris. One day.'

Silence.

'*Ma cocotte*,' Vivi turned around to face her sister. *Ma cocotte*. An endearment, spoken with affection. Catherine was taken aback. This was not like Vivi.

'I don't know how else to explain,' Vivi continued. 'When Georges abandoned us, I was seven years old – you were three. I could remember, I was old enough to ask. Marthe told me Georges might as well be dead, that's what she kept repeating. For me, it wasn't important. I was never close to him, I hardly remembered him. He wasn't around much when we were very young either, but you wouldn't have known that. I suppose I was coloured by Marthe's impressions. You are when you are a child. Over time it just became the story she told. I didn't challenge it. One didn't challenge a woman like Marthe. But you were too young to remember, so you were told the easy story. Perhaps she knew you would never be satisfied if she told you the truth, that you'd pester her to find him. I don't know. That's how I explain it. It wasn't a *deliberate* plan of deception, but once it became her story, I admit, it was hard to turn around.'

Catherine leant against the balustrade, closed her eyes, let the night air brush her skin. Was that the real story? Or just how Vivi saw it, or Marthe? Perhaps, now, she'd never know. In the end, what difference did it make? Or more importantly, even if it made a difference, did it really *matter*? Perhaps that was the question.

'Okay,' she said. 'It's okay.'

'I don't know what else to say. I'm . . . sorry that you were so upset.'

'You know, Vivi,' said Catherine suddenly. 'He had a newspaper cutting about me. Louise found it in his flat.'

Vivi clasped her, or perhaps Catherine clasped her sister first, she couldn't tell; whichever, it was clumsy.

'I must go now,' said Vivi, breaking away.

'I'll let you. Vivi . . .'

'Yes?'

'I think Henri might be able to take us to the airport.'

In the half-light Catherine could see her sister's taut face break into a smile.

'Perfect. I guessed as much. I'll see you in the morning, then.'

Lunch, on Henri's recommendation, was at the restaurant over-looking the town. They had a table on the terrace surrounding the pool. It was quiet; the waiters wordlessly efficient, the only sounds the slow, regular splashes of pre-lunch bathers in the pool.

'So, I was right to insist, to bring your sister to you? And, so obligingly, to take her to the airport?' Henri said. 'Come on, you must acknowledge.'

Catherine looked out across the collection of buildings, old and new, to the blue bay with its dotted islands beyond. She smiled. The journey to Tontouta had been a confusing comedy of slapstick and sentimentality. Vivi's luggage tumbling off the trolley, the five bags of duty free, the boutique collection, the perfume, the whisky for Vincent.

'My sister has never been real to me. She's like a caricature. And yet, for the first time today I kissed her goodbye with the thought that I might see her again soon. She called me *ma cocotte* and said we hadn't finished our conversations. I suppose I have you, partly, to thank for that.'

Henri smiled. 'Go on,' he said.

'Vivi at least grew up with the facts of the matter. Is that worse or better than to grow up without them, of always somehow knowing there was something missing?'

'I suppose that is for you to understand, one day. Have you considered that your life with Marthe might not have been as fulfilling as you might have imagined? Perhaps not packed with enriching, joyous experiences.'

Since her last conversation with Vivi, Catherine had tried to imagine it. Her mother and her sister, histrionically feuding with one another, as long as the day. Where would *she* have fitted in to all that, with her quiet manners, her aversion to conflict?

She sighed. 'Maybe Vivi was right.'

'And maybe your mother was astute enough to recognise that you were potentially more resilient. A survivor.'

Catherine was touched by the compliment, not sure if she could assimilate it yet into her changing view of herself.

'Perhaps.' It felt like a huge departure from what she had always believed. 'Perhaps.'

Henri allowed her the moment. 'So what is next for you?'

Catherine drew in her breath. 'You don't think I should contact the Naudins?'

He did not answer immediately, turning to the view, a frown settling on his face. 'I would be wary. They have been badly traumatised by the whole affair. They would not want reminders.'

'Maybe not. But maybe. It might be a comfort – a connection.'

Henri looked back down at the table, his expression guarded. 'I know people here, Catherine. What their political persuasion is, and so on. I would be cautious. You could write, I suppose. But . . .'

'What about the *tribu*?'

'Well, again, you could visit. I could help you, or perhaps you could arrange it through Adèle in Bourail. But remember,

Catherine, you do not know the ways of the clans here. It is sensitive. There's no guarantee that you would be welcomed, as a half-sister, even *that* unconfirmed. You understand what you represent, of course?'

'Yes, I know. It's maybe not a very good idea.'

'And Georges?'

'For Georges, it is a dead end. All I know is that my mother told me he didn't die. She didn't keep in touch with him. For Marthe, he was absolutely dead. Gone, disappeared. For Vivi too.'

'Why do you want to find him, Catherine?'

She looked up at him, surprised. 'Well, that's why I'm here, isn't it?'

'Is it?'

She couldn't answer. He waited, watching her face.

'What kind of a man do you really think he *was*, Catherine?'

Still she said nothing. Henri could see he had disturbed her. She had lowered her eyes, planted her elbows on the table. She had that brooding look he was starting to know.

'I don't know, Henri.'

She was not ready, he understood. Perhaps it was too soon, too much.

'I have another idea,' he said. 'I should have said before. Perhaps, have you thought, he is in Australia?'

Catherine looked up again. 'You're right. I had thought of that. I could try to track him down back home.'

'I knew . . . you would have to leave . . .' said Henri. 'If not back to Australia, to France.'

Catherine shook her head, not quite believing she had heard him correctly. But she had. Time to stop running. To stop pretending.

'I'm not ready to leave. Not my story – nor you, not yet.'

She reached out for his hand across the table, knocking her wine glass over in a memory of less certain times.

Twenty-three

Dear Madame,

It was with a great deal of surprise that I received your letter just yesterday. At first, I have to tell you, it was something of a shock – but I decided to write immediately because it seems that finally we may be able to put together some of the missing pieces of my son's life.

As you have discovered we now live in Nouméa, but Gaëtan spends most of the week, sometimes even the weekend, on his brother-in-law's property outside of Nouméa. I have to warn you that my husband and I do not feel the same way about the events surrounding Robert's death. Since we left Panié, Gaëtan has said not a single word about the incident, and has not so much as mentioned Robert's name. We have no photos in our house, all his personal effects have been disposed of, except some of his workbooks from school and some personal letters. They were, I am afraid to say, destined for the bonfire. Forgive me for my frankness, it is not usual for me, but I have been living for so long in the shadow of his grief that until your letter of hope I was not sure I would ever be able to surface from it. Gaëtan has not seen your letter and I am reluctant to show it to him, as I am sure he will not be able to respond positively. I am sorry, but this is his way.

For my part I would be very glad to meet with you. There is much to tell. You would need to visit during the week when Gaëtan is away, as I do not plan to let him know. It would be best if you telephoned on a weekday and we can try to arrange something.

For me personally I am very touched by your gesture, and I am thankful to you for your courage in writing to us.

With my sincere best wishes,

Dominique Naudin

Dominique Naudin's house was to the north of the town, in a suburb called la Vallée des Colons. Set back a little from the street, almost concealed behind a hibiscus hedge, Catherine could make out the shutters across the front of the house, badly in need of a coat of paint, and the familiar red of a rusted corrugated-iron roof. It was three-thirty – afternoon tea, she guessed. Time enough to talk without imposing.

The door opened and they were face to face. Did you shake hands or embrace? The woman at the door had her hand outstretched, welcoming.

Catherine took one of her hands, then grasped both. Looked into her face, tried to read the emotion.

'*Entrez, entrez,*' said Dominique. She smiled a little nervously and ushered Catherine through the house to the deck.

'We'll sit outside, please, just kick off the cat. *Allez,* Minouche! *Hop!*'

She indicated a teak chair, warmed by the sun and the now-stretching cat, next to a table on which was arranged an assortment of small patisseries, two teacups, milk jug and silver sugar bowl.

Catherine sat down and looked out over the small back garden, which sloped upwards to another hibiscus hedge. Between the yellow flowers she could make out the familiar shape of a Melanesian woman moving slowly, hanging out clothes.

'Hard to get used to neighbours, Gaëtan can't abide them,' Dominique was saying. To their left was a small aviary where a dozen little red finches hopped and squeaked. 'The remains of my menagerie. We had so many animals . . . You'll have tea?'

'Yes, yes, of course.'

Dominique disappeared back inside, returning with the teapot. Silence as she poured. Catherine cleared her throat.

'I'm very touched that you have invited me here today, Madame Naudin. I – '

'I can see you are his sister,' Dominique interrupted abruptly. 'Seeing you here now, I am struck by . . . the resemblance. As simple as that, a true thread.' She covered her mouth with her hands for a brief moment, then took them away, smiling through tears. 'Call me Dominique, please.'

'I didn't know of my brother's existence, Dominique, I – '

'Of course. I will get them, the photos, please excuse me a minute.'

Catherine took a cube of sugar, balanced it between forefinger and thumb in her tea, watched the amber seep into the white and dissolve away.

'Our farm,' said Dominique, returning with a newspaper cutting. Catherine peered. She expected to see the same cutting, the one Henri had brought to her. But this one had photos of the shell of the farmhouse at Panié, its roof a burnt curl of corrugated iron. Photos of Dominique being interviewed by gendarmes, of Gaëtan in a solemn embrace with an old Melanesian farmhand while a woman, also Melanesian, looked on. 'Oukanou, and his wife,' said Dominique, pointing. 'We called her Tante Lucie. She died not long after.'

'*Deux couleurs de peau – un même chagrin,*' Catherine read the caption underneath. 'Two skin colours – a common grief.'

'And here,' said Dominique, tapping on the other side of the paper. 'This is Robert.'

Over the page was a photo, framed in oval, of a young man. *Robert Naudin, 18 years old: died defending the Naudin property.*

There he was. Young. Wavy hair, light-brown perhaps. Smooth young skin – hard to see what colour. The irony of this obituary, you couldn't tell whether he was black or white.

I've seen him before, I'm sure, she thought. Or is it just that there *is* a resemblance?

'Please tell me about him.'

'Oh,' breathed Dominique, relieved to break the tension. 'Where should I start?'

She waited as Dominique sifted through the grains of a young lifetime, looking for something on which to build her construction. 'When he came to us at three, maybe four years, he smiled at me,' she said finally. 'After all he'd been through, he still had a smile. It's what is left, now, for me – that smile and that . . . spirit.'

As Dominique talked, the afternoon sun slid over the house, deepening the patch of sky they could see from the deck. Catherine heard the stories of his childhood, the familiar, the typical, the extraordinary, the ordinary. A childhood like so many others and yet exceptional, made unique in the telling, coloured by small details that differentiate an individual from any other. Dominique spoke for an hour, an hour and a half, needing no prompting.

'And the people who did this,' Catherine said. 'What has become of them?'

Dominique drew in her breath.

'There's no doubt the invasion was politically motivated. By members of the *tribu* surrounding our property. Around us, they were all pro-independence.'

'They were not members of his own *tribu* though? Surely not?'

'No, no, thank goodness, they live further down the coast. That would have been even more difficult to deal with. It could easily have been, though, had their land bordered ours. Robert's *tribu* was a strong FLNKS voice in the region. Gaëtan could never deal with that. Here, *en brousse*, you see, people do not see the problem in shades of grey, not those of our generation. For them there is no middle ground.'

She paused as the cat leapt up onto her lap. 'No, the people who did this can't have known that it was Robert who was on the property, the boy who so unfortunately switched on the torch that night. It was an act against what we represented, not the individuals who made up our family. It is only with the passage of time that I can see this. At the time you are too full of grief and hatred of those who did it. I say hatred because I am a mother, and these people killed my son. And even saying it I am filled with a mixture of anger and grief and regret because I ask myself again and again – if it were not for Gaëtan, perhaps, Robert might not have stayed with us, might have returned to his *tribu*, might not have been there on the night.'

'But had it not been for you, he would not have survived at all, would not have had the benefit of your care for his eighteen years,' protested Catherine.

'Perhaps. Yes. Of course, you torture yourself with these questions: if only this, if only that.' Dominique stopped, suddenly distracted by the observation that the tea had gone cold.

'No, no, don't get up,' said Catherine. 'So it was about claims to land, in the end, the incident on your farm?'

'In the end, yes,' answered Dominique. 'At first you cannot get past the personal. You see, I knew there were grudges against –

well, against Gaëtan and his alliances. But in the end, when you stand back, it really *was* about land, about recognition, about re-claiming what had been taken from them, back in colonial times. We here in New Caledonia have reached some under-standings, but much more is needed, compromise on both parts. I understand these things only because I have been forced to, because if you do not try to understand, then things do not evolve. I have learnt that we must move on in our thinking. But my husband will not agree, and it is too late for him to change, I think, now . . .'

She stroked the cat, who started up a loud purr. 'Not long after the event on our farm, they signed the agreements in Paris – *Les accords de Matignon*. Tjibaou, the Kanak leader and Lafleur, for the loyalists. You have seen the famous photo of them shaking hands. At the time I was too angry, too full of grief to follow what was happening. They came to a compromise, divided the country into provinces, recognised everyone's rights, gave amnesty for all preceding political events – excluding murder. But they never classified our event – whether the shots were premeditated or in fear of reprisal. Robert and his step-brothers – who were also injured – had their guns with them you see. So the presumed perpetrators of Robert's death were released. Gaëtan is pursuing it. But as for me,' she stopped again. 'As for me, I think you have to find your own meanings. I don't know if our system of justice will do that for me. What do you think, Minouche?' she said to the cat, who, jumping off her lap, appeared to stop and gaze out to the garden, as if considering the question.

'You cannot hope to understand it if you have not lived through it,' she continued. 'I do not want to trouble you with the details.' She stood abruptly and Catherine wondered if it was time to go.

'Wait. I'll show you something else.'

Catherine picked up the photo of Robert. She was sure she had seen him before.

Dominique reappeared and handed Catherine a folded sheet of paper. 'Go on,' she said. 'Read it.'

The looping handwriting, raw and intimate, was written on graph paper torn from an exercise book, the same kind she remembered from the convent school.

Assignment – *Littérature*. Robert Naudin

'Imagine you are the Little Prince writing to his friend after his death. What would you say?'

Dear Friend,

I am writing this letter to show you that I am not dead. People think that death is the end but you know, it's not true.

I still exist, but I have changed.

But this is not the only reason I've written you this letter. You know, when you drew the muzzle on my sheep, you forgot to add the leather thong. Don't worry, there's no problem. If I had a muzzle for my sheep, I would become lazy and I wouldn't be responsible for my rose. And that is very important. You have to risk pain if you want to be responsible for something. If you don't risk anything, you will never live.

I'm sending you this letter with a migration of birds, so I don't know when you will receive it. For this reason, I want to remind you of a few things. Remember the fox? The one who said 'l'essentiel est invisible aux yeux' – 'the most important things are invisible to the eye'. Remember, he said, it's the time you have lost for your rose that makes your rose so important.

He told me that he will always remember me by the golden colour of the wheat.

I hope that you will always remember me by the stars.

Ton bonhomme,

The Little Prince.

'He sent this to Rosina after her mother died,' said Dominique. 'She returned it to me because she thought I would find some comfort in it. Do you remember *Le Petit Prince*?

'Yes. I remember the rose,' said Catherine. She watched as Dominique took back the paper, folded it, turned her eyes to the hedge above, to the aviary.

Silence, before she dared to ask: 'Who was Rosina?'

'Rosina – she was Robert's girlfriend.'

'Is she . . . where does – ' started Catherine.

'She lives up on the east coast, with her family, unless she has moved. Sadly I have lost touch with her. Here, I meant to find her photo for you. I keep them away. Gaëtan is – well, it is difficult for him, still difficult.'

In the darkening light Catherine was glad of the comfort of the cat who had now taken up on her lap. Dominique returned with another photo and some folded letters.

'Here. Letters they sent to each other when Robert was at school over on the west coast. Ordinary, sweet letters. About dancing and homework and school. And her photo. Beautiful, isn't she? I lost touch with her after we moved, it is a way to travel and she has no telephone. Rosina has all her family up there, except her mother, who was killed in a road accident, about nine or ten years ago. Robert sent his *Little Prince* assignment to her after it happened. I don't think he knew how else to express his sadness, for her, for everyone. He couldn't say it directly. And now, it's as if – this is from him to us.'

'My mother died recently too,' Catherine blurted, then winced. She had not even responded to Dominique's loss, nor to this new connection, at once exciting and tragic. Dominique took her hand.

'Then you will understand.'

Catherine nodded, feeling the tears sting her eyes. Thinking that she couldn't possibly touch the grief of this woman facing her, nor that of the young, strong woman whose photo had to be hidden in their house, who had lost a mother and a boyfriend in the space of a few years.

Marthe. You were supposed to grieve when your mother died. What had she felt? What did she feel?

'I'm not sure I do understand what you've been through.'

'L'essentiel est invisible aux yeux,' said Dominique. 'The most important things are invisible to the eye. You can't even talk about them. You only feel them. I know that you will feel the same as me in the end, though we've arrived there on different roads.'

Catherine looked at her, incredulous.

'Thank you, Dominique. I feel as if I have known you for years.'

'I am so glad you came. I would like to see you again.'

'Of course. Au revoir, then.'

'Yes. A bientôt.'

'A bientôt.'

The markets at the Baie de la Moselle, open from early in the morning, were not usually a place to bump into people. Catherine had gone on a whim; it was a beautiful morning, her mind had been racing and she'd been unable to fall back to sleep past five o'clock. What she wanted now was time to sit outside and watch the world again, to reflect and plan the next stage.

She found a bench back from the action of the market, sat and tilted her head in the early sun, closed her eyes, pictured a grid with neat questions in each square. Sister – reconciliation, moderately successful. Must return at some stage to finalise papers. Half-brother – deceased but hopeful connection with adoptive mother. Search for more family up the coast? Mother – forgiven? This one had no clear answer so she moved to the next square.

Father – blank. Maybe some hope of finding him back in Australia? Next square – Henri? *Et Henri?*

Catherine stood up and looked out at the bay, its blue-azure mimicking the blue of the market building rooves. Yes, she had been here before, she was sure now. But the buildings hadn't been there, they had changed. The memory was of some small comfort.

She considered whether she might walk a little, having no answers in her last square. She took a step forward, dropping her eyes back to the ground to avoid the white glare of the water, and almost collided with a young man just crossing her path.

'Oh, *excusez-moi*, Madame. But it's Madame!'

Catherine looked into the young man's face, surprised at his instant recognition when she couldn't place him at all.

'Emmanuel, you know, Emmanuel from the hotel,' the man said.

'Oh, of course! How are you?'

'Well, I'm very well. And you, you also are much better I think, Madame? Much happier?'

'Oh, yes,' said Catherine, nodding automatically, yet not sure she could confirm the sentiment. Emmanuel had that kind of energetically polite style that pre-supposed everyone else to be feeling the same way as you.

'That's good, then,' said Emmanuel, and she sensed that the niceties were about to end. They shook hands, and Emmanuel stepped away with his bags of produce.

She stood, smiling a little as he walked away, thinking back to how he had teased her in that knowing sort of way, as if he had been privy to the drama of her stay. She wondered now if, by virtue of the gossip channels known as *radio-cocotier* he *had* followed her story. She almost wanted to take up the conversation again, to see what she might glean from him. Impulsively she opened her mouth to call his name and was surprised to see him turn around, as if in anticipation.

'Madame,' he said. 'I'm sure I will see you around again.'

'I hope so. I'm leaving for a trip tomorrow up the east coast,' she answered. 'When we get back perhaps I'll call by.'

Emmanuel inclined his head politely, the corners of a smile forming about his mouth; perhaps, she wondered, at her not-so-subtle reference to *we*.

'So I will be seeing you again soon, then,' he said.

'I think so. *Au revoir*,' answered Catherine, with an inward smile.

Twenty-four

Afterwards, she would remember the east coast journey as a play of light and dark; as if the shadows on the mountains had finally lifted, broken the clouds, rinsed the valleys with rain.

Henri arrived for her in the four-wheel-drive. As they passed onto the toll-road Catherine wound down her window, felt the warm air on her skin, watched the grey kilometres uncoil behind. She wondered what had conspired to bring her this pure moment and closed her eyes a second to take it in.

Henri played the tourist guide to perfection. They stopped for coffee in Boulouparis, bought flowers from the market in Bourail. Catherine wanted to backtrack to the beach at La Roche Percée. And Turtle Bay, insisted Henri, seeing as they were late already. They looked down on the bay framed at the top by its tall colonial pines, the slender columnar trees which Henri told her were used to make the outriggers seen in all the tourist brochures. The Kanak symbol for male, yet they curved gracefully towards each other, their tips almost touching.

She thought she could see a turtle in the sea but Henri told her they would have to come early to watch them climb up the beach. They called in on Marie-Claude, *last stop* said Henri, *or we won't make it before nightfall.* Catherine had a thank-you letter for Dr Bernard.

'Go and disturb him at the clinic,' urged Marie-Claude. But today he was not to be disturbed. A birth had become complicated and the mother would have to be evacuated to Nouméa. Catherine left him the letter, disappointed.

Finally they took the Col des Rousettes to the other side of the island. Here the *caldoches* ate red bat stew, Henri told her solemnly. He had to be joking, no self-respecting Frenchman would eat bats, stewed, pickled or baked into a terrine. But they are not really French, are they? They are *New Caledonians*.

The vegetation transformed from dry to wet, the paddocks and cattle enclosures giving way to the green forests and streams of the *chaîne*.

Henri fiddled with tapes of Brassens and Brel, '*un grand sentimental*, unashamedly,' trying to steer at the same time until Catherine slapped his fingers and took over, fumbling for some female singers in his collection. She smiled to discover old tapes of Dusty Springfield in the box and settled finally on Françoise Hardy.

'What was that?' Catherine said abruptly. 'We passed something. Can we stop?'

Henri braked. 'I'm not sure you will want to see it.'

It was the shell of a house. They stepped through the doorway. The late afternoon sun slanted through the space where once had been a front door; vines strangled the open frames of the windows. The walls were singed with black, smeared over with graffiti old and new. Broken glass littered the floor and there was the smell of urine, rats, decay.

Catherine bent to scrub away the dirt concealing the tiles, which, though chipped, revealed a pattern of *fleur de lys* in faded colours of burgundy and blue. A surge of recognition washed over her. *Chez les bonnes soeurs.* The same ones, in the convent school.

Henri had fallen silent. Catherine glanced across at him, staring through the gaps between the burnt and rotted louvres of the shutters. *'Le flamboyant,'* he said, indicating the tree. 'There, in the garden. It is still flowering.' He turned to Catherine, his hands in his pockets. 'I can't remember who lived here.'

Catherine took a step towards the window. 'Poinciana,' she said, looking out. 'A friend has one in her garden, in Queensland. She calls it *red fire*. It blooms in December.'

'Red fire,' said Henri quietly. 'Yes, fire in December.'

'Let's go,' said Catherine. 'I've seen enough.'

They reached the other side of the pass, the start of the coast road. The road wound along the coastline, providing glimpses of blue through the dense green.

'It is hard to accept the violence,' Henri took up. 'From a distance, hard also to understand the positions. New Caledonia is one of the last of France's colonial outposts. You can imagine why she would not let her island go graciously. No, it was not gracious – violence never is. Not for anyone, whatever their position.'

'But what do you think? Were they justified? The Kanaks – to push out the *caldoches* so violently?'

'Were the *colons* justified, in exploiting the Kanak territory?' Henri countered quickly. 'Do you imagine colonisation happened peaceably? There was bloodshed on both sides. It is a question, in the end, of whether you think violence is *ever* justified as a means to an end. It is easy to distance yourself from the issue. You do not live with the threat of *your* house being taken over. My guess is you would use violence to protect yourself if it happened.'

They drove on into the dusk. Catherine said nothing, stirred by the image of the burnt-out, derelict house, trying to understand the conflict. The article Henri had published following Robert's shooting – written to inspire compassion in the hardest of pro-independent hearts. And yet he had so many contacts with the Kanak community; he had so easily arranged their invitation to stay in the *tribu* tonight. He defended their position, despite the stance of the paper that paid his salary.

Henri dropped one hand from the steering wheel, finding hers.

'What are you thinking?'

'I don't know what to think. It seems so – *wrong* and yet at the same time – it's understandable. It was like that for Robert's family, wasn't it?'

He shrugged, gave a barely perceptible nod, squeezed her hand.

'It's painful for me then too,' she continued. 'I'm a part of this – of them, of the whole thing.'

'We are all a part of it. See it that way. But part of something else too. You might call it the future. You also have to see it like that.' He shot her a glance. 'Almost there now.'

At right angles to the horizon, the rain clouds blurred against a deepening backdrop of sea-sky. A silhouette of pandanus emerged starkly in the foreground, like a black motif painted on a cloak of silver-white rays.

'I'm still not sure about sleeping on a reed mat,' she said. 'Do they have mosquito zappers in their huts?

'We'll see,' said Henri.

The evening, everything about it, was simple. They were greeted by the *chef* and some of the women, presented their gifts. Catherine had brought patisseries for the children; Henri, money and cigarettes. *His* cigarettes, she wondered. She hadn't noticed him reaching for them all day.

In the end, no one spoke of Robert, of a possible connection. It was better. They were visitors, guests, observers, partakers of an exchange.

They bathed at the river just as the moon rose. They ate a simple meal, prepared and served by one of the women: chicken with yams and banana, salad of chokos and sliced raw paw-paw. Dessert was pineapple, sweet and golden.

Present happiness. Wasn't it usually a memory? Could you not try to gather it, hold it in your hand, or pocket it, small as a coffee bean, to know it was always there?

'When I first met you, Henri, I – ' she started.

'You did not know what to make of me.'

'I still don't.'

Henri raised his eyebrows.

'Good.'

'What do you mean, good?'

'I mean, it will take more time to know me. You will need a little more time.'

She couldn't read his face. The expression had been teasing, but now creased into something graver. She held his eyes, returning their intimacy. She knew then that he too had his story, put on hold, and for a second felt grateful that he had let her bare hers first.

'Thank you for bringing me here.'

'You needed to come.'

'I know. You understood. Thank you.'

Henri drew her to him in a band of tight emotion. And as certainly as she was uncertain before, though she had no sense of the form it would take, Catherine knew there would be a future.

The proximity of the sea brings back images to me; memories perhaps, or yearnings. My dreams now are for imagined, possible futures, no longer the past.

I have my sights fixed into the distance, though I have to shield my eyes from the sun. I see two blurred figures approaching. My heart quickens to discern first a child, a girl of six or seven, flitting like a swallow to the water's edge, then back to the form of a woman. The young girl fossicks in the sand, finds a treasure, shows the woman who stops to inspect, then takes up the pace again, steadily forward. The woman is carrying shoes, her own and the girl's. She has her eyes on the sand, seems thoughtful. The girl faces the sea and the huge grey sky, dares the waves to lap her feet, races away. She laughs triumphantly in that timeless action of children on the edges of every country in the world. Her mane of hair ripples, springy and thick, the colour of burnished gold. Her teeth are white against her honey skin. Taking the woman's hand, she pulls her forward now, impatiently. The woman looks up as if remembering something, and sees me ahead. She waves; I know she is expecting me. The child pulls down the woman's neck, whispers something to her ear. Hurry, I think. *Hurry.*

And then they are *there.* 'Rosina, it's Catherine. It's so good to be here, to meet you.'

'And who are you?' I squat to look into the girl's face. She lifts it in the familiar gesture of embrace, a kiss on each cheek.

'This is my daughter, Aimata,' says Rosina. 'Aimata, this is Catherine.'

'Can I call her *tantine?*' says the child.

'Of course,' I say, touched, suddenly overcome by the gesture. I can't help reaching to caress Aimata's hair, chuck her under the chin. The girl smiles openly, in the way children touched by gentleness can smile. We link arms, make our way back up the beach, across the road to the house.

They left early in the morning after breakfast, quietly. After a few hours Henri turned left onto a dirt road.

It was not advisable to visit. Gaëtan's property had been reclaimed, though nobody could determine exactly who had taken up occupation. It was still not considered safe to travel here, especially if you were not a local. Some areas were just out of bounds – tribal lands, private areas of spiritual significance. Henri had taken advice, he said, from those who were in a position to advise.

'We'll see how far we get,' he'd told Catherine.

The road wound along the valley, rising above the river and dipping to its level, for a while running parallel to the bamboo-lined banks. Mist spread like clotted milk over the water; from a height bisecting the morning into white and green. It had been a good season for rain, the new growth was everywhere lush and verdant. They drove past old coffee plantations, the delicate coffee trees sheltering under broad-leafed ironwood, past groves of banana and paw-paw trees, every now and again glimpsing well-tended terraces of yam and taro through clear-ings. Horses were as common as cows along this road and several times they surprised them in the middle of the road, old dusty mares wandering free or bad-tempered mules tethered on ropes.

Neither spoke. Catherine sensed the calm of the valley to be at odds with the intensity of its recent past. She felt there might be a point when she would want to say *Stop. Turn around. Go back*, but strangely, it didn't come. She expected to encounter someone, anyone, at every bend in the road, and the anticipation of this made her feel tense. But the road was deserted. Even early, when a half-day's work could be finished, not a soul crossed their path.

Until just before they reached the farm. Henri recognised what was coming, from the sudden appearance of the irregular fence lines of gaiac and old wire. He slowed as he perceived a figure fifty metres ahead. A young Kanak riding bareback on a horse. Over his shoulder slung a rifle.

Henri rolled down his window as they approached.

'*Ciaou.*'

The man raised his eyebrows in acknowledgement but gave no reply.

'We're just touring – a *poken* next to me,' Henri said, indicating Catherine. 'Okay to come here?'

The young man pulled the horse around. He shrugged. 'The *chef*, that way.' He gestured vaguely towards a small path leading off the road.

'How far?'

'*Là-bas,*' answered the man. 'Down there. Go see him.'

'Okay, thank you. Good day, Monsieur,' said Henri. 'We'll turn back, I think,' he said under his breath. He looked across at Catherine. 'I don't think we'll see the farm today. I'm sorry. I just don't think it's a good idea.'

'It's okay,' said Catherine, exhaling a slow breath of tension. 'It's enough.'

'I hope you're not too hungry. There won't be a coffee for another fifty kilometres.'

'Let's keep moving,' said Catherine.

The four-wheel-drive was at the edge of the river, waiting for the ferry to return with its heavy load. Six cars; unusual for this time of the year, mid-week, mid-January.

There were not so many going in the opposite direction, up the island, for there was nothing now until the remote towns of Pouébo, and Ouégua. Not much interest for mainstream tourists; most of them didn't visit during the cyclone season anyway. Catherine was nervous but Henri joked that the swim would be pleasant if the car fell in.

They caught a glimpse of the cascade before the bridge, then Henri pulled up in front of a bare cement dwelling hidden behind a clump of banana trees. A hand-painted sign indicated a fee of 200 francs was required to access the track. Catherine could find no one to answer the door so pushed some coins under it.

The path wound through the rainforest, emerging suddenly to the roar of the white water. The luxuriance of the vegetation was almost an assault on the senses; so lush, so dense. As they approached they could no longer hear each other, but there was no need for words.

There it was, the waterfall they called Tao. Once used, so Henri told her, to drive a small hydro-electric plant to smelter blocks of ferro-nickel.

His sights fixed on the highest rock pool, Henri gestured for her to follow.

Epilogue

A taxi pulls up before the departures entrance at Coolangatta airport. The passenger is a thin man in his seventies with a pocked, greyish face. He has some difficulty removing the seat belt and extricating his legs. Once on the pavement he organises his small case. The taxi driver offers to help but the man waves him on. He walks, a little unsteadily, in the direction of the automatic doors, looking uncomfortable in his crisp blue shirt and new, too-baggy trousers. Half-way across the pedestrian crossing he stops and stoops down, hovering over a flash of gold on the bitumen. The taxis rev impatiently as he retrieves the coin and tucks it into his pocket. He disappears, sucked into the blackness of the terminal building.

Inside, he finds the right check-in desk and sends his case off. He needs some smokes. He'll buy a paper as well. There's just time for a drink; he'll head for the bar.

On his way he stops, as if he has suddenly seen himself in a mirror, though there are no mirrors. He turns, finds a seat and positions himself on it, sitting upright, staring ahead. He seems after a while to be stuck in this straight-ahead position, as if he cannot look sideways; neither right nor left.

Over the loudspeaker they are calling his name. He has time for a drink. He'll head for the bar. They are calling his name.

On second thoughts, he will sit here a while.

Last call for Flight 257 to Sydney. Will all remaining passengers for Flight 257 please proceed immediately to Gate 3 as the plane is now ready for departure.

He will sit here a while.

Perhaps he'll catch the next one.

Il n'y eut rien qu'un éclair jaune près de sa cheville. Il demeura un instant
immobile. Il ne cria pas. Il tomba doucement comme tombe un arbre.
Ça ne fit même pas de bruit, à cause du sable.

Nothing but a flash of yellow close to his ankle.
He remained motionless for an instant. He did not cry out.
He fell as gently as a tree falls. Not even a sound,
because of the sand.

Le Petit Prince
Antoine de Saint Exupéry, 1958

Acknowledgements

I am indebted to the following people for their contribution towards the realisation of this novel. To Nicholas Jose for his belief that it could happen, expert guidance and encouragement. To Pip Milroy for her interest, support and painstaking reading of the early drafts. To Suzie Grano for her indefatigable attention to detail and specialist knowledge in so many areas. To Penny Smith for her close editing. To Françoise Piron, typo-spotter extraordinaire. To Michou, Domi, Hervé, Honoré and Laura for inspiration. To Colette Mrowa-Hopkins for her advice on the use of the French. To Alex Hester, for permission to use her Year 11 French assignment based on Le Petit Prince. To my readers: Jan Turner, Sandy Clark, Daniel Ransan, Kris Paul, Carmel Hemmings, Blandine Stefanson, a big thank you. To my editor Gina Inverarity for her insightful reading, constructive suggestions and forbearance of eleventh-hour alterations. To the team at Wakefield Press: Julia, Stephanie and Michael for providing perspective, realism and spirited debate and to Liz for her superb cover design.

I am grateful to ArtsSA for an emerging artist's grant that

enabled me to concentrate on the early draft for four almost-uninterrupted months. And finally to my family for their frequent interruptions and tolerance, a big thank you.